T
la
pe

•
•

CONVENIENTLY WED TO THE PRINCE

CONVENIENTLY WED TO THE PRINCE

NINA MILNE

MILLS & BOON

First published in Great Britain 2018
by Mills & Boon, an imprint of HarperCollins*Publishers*
1 London Bridge Street, London, SE1 9GF

Large Print edition 2019

© 2018 Nina Milne

ISBN: 978-0-263-07892-3

MIX
Paper from
responsible sources
FSC C007454

This book is produced from independently certified
FSC™ paper to ensure responsible forest management.
For more information visit www.harpercollins.co.uk/green.

Printed and bound in Great Britain
by CPI Group (UK) Ltd, Croydon, CR0 4YY

This book is for my lovely parents,
who made my childhood a happy place.

Thank you!

PROLOGUE

*Eighteen months ago, Il Boschetto di Sole—
a lemon grove situated in the mountains of
Lycander*

HOLLY ROMANO STARED at her reflection. The
dress was ivory perfection, a bridal confection
of froth and lace, beauty and elegance, and she
loved it. Happiness bubbled inside her—this
was the fairy tale she'd dreamed of, the happy-
ever-after she'd vowed would be hers. She and
Graham were about to embark on a marriage as
unlike her parents' as possible—a partnership
of mutual love.

Not for Holly the bitterness and constant re-
crimination—a union based on the drear of duty
on her father's part and the daily misery of unrequited love on her mother's. Their marriage
had eventually shattered, and in the final con-
fetti shards of acrimony her mother had walked
away and never come back. Leaving eight-year-

old Holly behind without so much as a backward glance.

Holly pushed the images from her mind—she only wanted happy thoughts today, so she reminded herself of her father's love. A love she valued with all her heart because, although he never spoke of it, she knew of his disappointment that Holly had not been the longed-for son. And yet he had never shown her anything but love. Unlike her mother, who had never got over the bitter let-down of her daughter's gender and had never shown Holly even an iota of affection, let alone love.

Enough. Happy thoughts, remember?

Such as her additional joy that her father wholeheartedly approved of his soon-to-be son-in-law. Graham Salani was the perfect addition to the Romano family—a man who worked the land and would be an asset to Il Boschetto di Sole, the lemon grove the Romano family had worked on for generations. For over a century the job of overseer had passed from father to son, until Holly had broken the chain. But now Graham would be the son her father had always wanted.

It was all perfect.

Holly smiled at her reflection and half turned as the door opened and her best friend Rosa came in. It took her a second to register that Rosa wasn't in her bridesmaid dress—which didn't make sense as the horse-drawn carriage was at the door, ready to convey them to the chapel.

'Rosa...?'

'Holly, I'm sorry. I can't go through with this. You need to know.' Rosa's face held compassion as she stepped forward.

'I don't understand.'

She didn't want to understand as impending knowledge threatened to make her implode. Suddenly the dress felt weighted, each pearl bead filled with lead, and the smile on her face froze into a rictus.

'What do I need to know?'

'Graham is having an affair.' Rosa stepped towards her, hand outstretched. 'He has been for the past year.'

'That's not true.'

It couldn't be. But why would Rosa lie? She was Graham's sister—Holly's best friend.

'Ask your father.'

The door opened and Thomas Romano entered.

Holly forced herself to meet her father's eyes, saw the truth there and felt pain lance her.

'Holly, it is true. I am sorry.'

'Are you sure?'

'Yes. I have spoken with Graham myself. He claims it meant nothing, that he still loves you, still wants you to marry him.'

Holly tried to think, tried to cling to the crumbling, fading fairy tale.

'I can't do that.'

How could she possibly marry a man who had cheated on her? When she had spent years watching the ruins of a marriage brought down by infidelity? In thought and intent if not in deed. Holly closed her eyes. She had been such a fool—she hadn't had an inkling, not a clue. Humiliation flushed her skin, seeped into her very soul.

Her father stepped towards her, placed an arm around her. 'I am so sorry.'

She could hear the pain in his voice, the guilt.

'I had no idea.'

'I know you didn't.'

Graham didn't love her. The bleak thought spread through her system and she closed her eyes, braced herself. An image of the chapel, the carefully chosen flowers, the rows of people, family and friends happy in anticipation, flashed across her mind.

'We need to cancel the wedding.'

CHAPTER ONE

Present day, Notting Hill, London

STEFAN PETRELLI, EXILED Prince of Lycander, pushed his half-eaten breakfast across the cherrywood table in an abrupt movement.

It was a lesson to him not to open his post whilst eating—though, to be fair, he could hardly have anticipated *this* letter. Sprinkled with legalese, it summoned him to a meeting at the London law offices of Simpson, Wright and Gallagher for the reading of a will.

The will of Roberto Bianchi, Count of Lycander.

Lycander—the place of Stefan's birth, the backdrop of a childhood he'd rather forget. The place he'd consigned to oblivion when he'd left aged eighteen, with his father's curses echoing in his ears.

'If you leave Lycander you will not be coming

back. I will take all your lands, your assets and privileges, and you will be an outcast.'

Just the mention of Lycander was sufficient to chase away his appetite and bring a scowl to his face—a grimace that deepened as he stared down at the document. The temptation to crumple it up and lob it into the recycling bin was childish at best, and at twenty-six he had thankfully long since left the horror of childhood behind.

What on earth could Roberto Bianchi have left him? And why? The Count had been his mother Eloise's godfather and guardian—the man who had allowed his ward to marry Stefan's father, Alphonse, for the status and privileges the marriage would bring.

What a disaster *that* had been. The union had been beyond miserable, and the ensuing divorce a medley of bitterness and humiliation with Stefan a hapless pawn. Alphonse might have been ruler of Lycander, but he had also been a first class, bona fide bastard, who had ground Eloise into the dust.

Enough. The memories of his childhood—the pain and misery of his father's *Toughen Stefan up and Make him a Prince* Regime, the enduring ache of missing his mother, whom he had only been allowed to see on infrequent occasions, his guilt at the growing realisation that his mother's plight was due to her love for *him* and the culminating pain of his mother's exile—could not be changed.

Alphonse was dead—had been for three years— and Eloise had died long before that, in dismal poverty. Stefan would never forgive himself for her death, and now Stefan's half-brother, Crown Prince Frederick, ruled Lycander.

Frederick. For a moment he dwelled on his older sibling. Alphonse had delighted in pitting his sons against each other, and as result there was little love lost between the brothers.

True, since he'd come to the throne Frederick had reached out to him—even offered to reinstate the lands, assets and rights Alphonse had stripped from him—but Stefan had refused. *Forget it. No way.* Stefan would never be beholden to a ruler of Lycander again and he would not return on his brother's sufferance.

He'd built his own life—left Lycander with an utter determination to succeed, to show his father, show Lycander, show the *world* what Stefan

Petrelli was made of. Now he was worth millions. He had built up a global property and construction firm. Technically, he could afford to buy up most of Lycander. In reality, though, he couldn't purchase so much as an acre—his father had passed a decree that banned Stefan from buying land or property there.

Stefan shook his head to dislodge the bitter memories—that way lay nothing but misery. His life was good, and he'd long ago accepted that Lycander was closed to him, so there was no reason to get worked up over this letter. He'd go and see what bequest had been left to him and he'd donate it to his charitable foundation. *End of.*

Yet foreboding persisted in prickling his nerve-endings as instinct told him that it wouldn't be that easy.

Holly Romano tucked a tendril of blonde hair behind her ear and stared at the impressive exterior of the offices that housed Simpson, Wright and Gallagher, a firm of lawyers renowned for their circumspection, discretion and the size of the fees they charged their often celebrity clientele.

Last chance to bottle it, and her feet threatened

to swivel her around and head her straight back to the tube station.

No. There was nothing to be afraid of. Roberto Bianchi had owned Il Boschetto di Sole. The Romano family had been employed by the Bianchis for generations and therefore Roberto had decided to leave Holly something. Hence the letter that had summoned her here to be told details of the bequest.

But it didn't make sense. Roberto Bianchi had been only a shadowy figure in Holly's life. In childhood he had seemed all-powerful as the owner of the place her family lived in and loved—a man known to be old-fashioned in his values, strict but fair, and a great believer in tradition. Owner of many vast lands and estates in Lycander, he had had a soft spot for Il Boschetto di Sole—the crown jewel of his possessions.

As an employer he had been hands-off,. He had trusted her father completely. And although he'd shown a polite interest in Holly he had never singled her out in any way. Plus she'd had no contact with him in the past eighteen months, since her decision to leave Lycander for a while.

The aftermath of her wedding fiasco had been

too much—the humiliation, the looks of either pity or censure, and the nagging knowledge that her father was disappointed. Not because he questioned her decision to cancel the wedding, but because it was his dream to see her happily married, to have the prospect of grandsons and the knowledge Romano traditions and legacies were secured.

There had also been her need to escape Graham. At first he had been contrite, in pursuit of reconciliation, but when she had declined to marry him his justifications had become cruel. Because he had never loved her. And eventually, at their last meeting, he had admitted it.

'I wooed you because I wanted promotion—wanted an in on the Romanos' wealth and position. I never loved you. You are so young, so inexperienced. And Bianca...she is all-woman.'

That had been the cruellest cut of all. Because somehow, especially when she had seen Bianca, a tiny bit of Holly hadn't blamed him. Bianca was not just beautiful, she seemed to radiate desirability, and seeing her had made Holly look back on her nights with Graham and cringe.

Even now, eighteen months later, standing on

a London street with the autumn breeze blowing her hair any which way, a flush of humiliation threatened as she recalled what a fool she had made of herself with her expressions of love and devotion, her inept fumbling. And the whole time Graham would have been comparing her to Bianca, laughing his cotton socks off.

Come on, Holly. Focus on the here and now.

And right now she needed to walk through the revolving glass door.

Three minutes later she followed the receptionist into the office of Mr James Simpson. It was akin to stepping into the past. The atmosphere was nigh on Victorian. Heavy tomes lined three of the panelled walls, and a portrait hung above the huge mahogany desk of a jowly, bearded, whiskered man from a bygone era. And yet she noticed that atop the desk there was a sleek state-of-the-art computer that indicated the law firm had at least one foot firmly in the current century.

A pinstripe-suited man rose to greet her: thin, balding, with bright blue eyes that shone with innate shrewd intelligence.

Holly moved forward with a smile, and as she did so her attention snagged on the other occupant of the room—a man who stood by the window, fingers drumming his thigh in a staccato burst that exuded an edge of impatience.

He was not conventionally handsome, in the drop-dead gorgeous sense, although there was certainly nothing wrong with his looks. A shade under six feet tall, he had dark unruly hair with a hint of curl, a lean face, a nose that jutted with intent and intense dark grey eyes under strong brows that pulled together in a frown.

Unlike Holly, he hadn't deemed the occasion worthy of formal wear and was dressed in faded jeans and a thick blue and green checked shirt over a white T-shirt. His build was lean and lithe, and whilst he wasn't built like a power house he emitted strength, and an impression that he propelled his way through life fuelled by sheer force of personality.

The man behind the desk cleared his throat and heat tinged her cheeks as she realised she had stopped dead in her tracks to gawp. She further realised that the object of her gawping looked somewhat exasperated. An expression that morphed into something else as he returned her gaze, studied her face with a dawning of...

Of what? Awareness? Arrest? Whatever it was, it sent a funny little fizz through her veins. Then his scowl deepened further, and quickly she turned away and resumed her progress towards the desk.

'Mr Simpson? I'm Holly Romano. Apologies for being a little late.' No need to explain the reason had been a sheer blue funk.

The lawyer looked at his watch, a courteous smile on his thin lips. 'Not a problem. I'm sure His Highness will agree.'

His Highness?

As her brain joined the dots and his identity dawned on her 'His Highness'—contrary to all probability—managed to look even grumpier as he pushed away from the wall.

'I don't use the title. Stefan is fine—or if you prefer to maintain formality go with Mr Petrelli.' A definitive edge tinged his tone and indicated that Stefan Petrelli felt strongly on the matter.

Stefan Petrelli. A wave of sheer animosity surprised her with its intensity as she surveyed the son of Eloise, one-time Crown Princess of Lycander. The very same Eloise whom her father had once loved, with a love that had infused her parents' marriage with bitterness and doomed it to joylessness.

As a child Holly had heard the name Eloise flung at her father in hatred time after time, until Eloise had haunted her dreams as the wicked witch of the Romano household, her shadowy ghostly presence a third person in her parents' marriage.

Of course she knew that this was not the fault of Stefan Petrelli, and furthermore Eloise was no longer a threat. The former Princess had died years before. Yet as she looked at him an instinctive visceral hostility still sparked. Her mother's words, screamed at her father, were still fresh in her head as they echoed down the tunnel of memories.

'Your precious Eloise with her son—something else she could have given you that I can't. That is what you want more than anything—a Stefan of your own.'

Those words had imbued her three-year-old self with an irrational jealousy of a boy she'd never met. Holly had wanted to be a boy so much she had ached with it. She had known how much both her parents had prayed for a boy, how bitterly disappointed they had been with a girl.

Her mother had never got over it, never forgiven her for her gender, and that knowledge was a bleak one that right now, rationally or not, added to the linger of a stupid jealousy of this man. It prompted her to duck down in a curtsey that she hoped conveyed irony. 'Your Highness,' she said, with deliberate emphasis.

His eyebrows rose and his eyes narrowed. 'Ms Romano,' he returned.

His deep voice ran over her skin, and before she could prevent it his hand had clasped hers to pull her up.

'You must have missed what I told Mr Simpson. I prefer not to use my title.'

Holly would have loved to have thought of a witty retort, but unfortunately her brain seemed unable to put together even a single syllable. Because her central nervous system seemed to have short-circuited as a result of his touch. Which was, of course, insane. Even with Graham this hadn't happened, so until now she would have pooh-poohed the idea of sparks and electric shocks as ridiculous figments of an overwrought imagination.

And yet the best her vocal cords could eventually manage was, 'Okey-dokey.'

Okey-dokey? For real, Holly?

With an immense effort she tugged her hand free and hauled herself together. 'Right. Um… Now introductions are over perhaps we could…?'

'Get down to business,' James Simpson interpolated. 'Of course. Please have a seat, both of you.'

In truth it was a relief to sink onto the surprisingly comfortable straight-backed chair. *Focus.*

James Simpson cleared his throat. 'Thank you for coming. Count Roberto wrote his will with both of you in mind. As you may or may not know, the bulk of his vast estate has gone to a distant Bianchi cousin, who will also inherit the title. However, I wish to speak to you about Count Bianchi's wishes with regards to Il Boschetto di Sole—the lemon grove he loved so much and where he spent a lot of the later years of his life. Holly's family, the Romanos, have lived on the grove for many generations, working the land.

And Crown Princess Eloise spent many happy times there before her marriage.'

Next to her Holly felt Stefan's body tense, almost as if that fact was news to him. She leant forward, her mind racing with curiosity.

James steepled his fingers together. 'In a nutshell, the terms of Roberto's will state that Il Boschetto di Sole will go to either one of you, dependent on which of you marries first and remains married for a year.'

Say what?

Holly blinked as her brain attempted to decode the words. Even as blind primitive instinct kicked in an image of the beauty of the land, the touch of the soil, the scent of lemons pervaded her brain. The Romanos had given heart and soul, blood and sweat to the land for generations. Stefan Petrelli had turned his back on Lycander. And yet if he married the grove would go to *him*, to Eloise's son. *No.*

Before she could speak, the dry voice of the lawyer continued.

'If neither of you has succeeded in meeting the criteria of the will in three years from this date Il Boschetto di Sole will go to the Crown—to

Crown Prince Frederick of Lycander or whoever is then ruler.'

There was a silence, broken eventually by Stefan Petrelli. 'That is a somewhat unusual provision.'

Was that all he could say? '"Unusual"?' Holly echoed. 'It's *ridiculous!*'

The lawyer looked unmoved by her comment. 'The Count has left you each a letter, wherein I assume he explains his decision. Can I suggest a short break? Mr Petrelli, if you'd care to read your letter in the annexe room to your left. Ms Romano, you can remain here.'

Reaching into his desk drawer, he pulled out two envelopes sealed with the Bianchi crest.

Stefan accepted his document and strode towards the door indicated by the lawyer. James Simpson then handed Holly hers and she waited until he left the room before she tugged it open with impatient fingers.

Dear Holly

You are no doubt wondering if I have lost my mind. Rest assured I have not. Il Boschetto di Sole is dear to my old-fashioned heart, and I want it to continue as it has for generations as an independent business.

The Bianchi heir is not a man I approve of, but I have little choice but to leave a vast amount of my estates to him. However, the grove is unentailed, and as he has made it clear to me that he would sell it to a corporation I feel no compunction in leaving Il Boschetto di Sole elsewhere.

But where? I have no children of my own and it is time to find a new family. I wish for Il Boschetto di Sole to pass from father and mother to son or daughter, for tradition to continue. So of course my mind goes to the Romanos, who have given so much to the land over the years.

You may be wondering why I have not simply left the grove to your father. Why I have involved Prince Stefan. To be blunt, your father is getting on, and his good health is in question. Once he is no longer on this earth Il Boschetto di Sole would go to you, and I do not know if that is what you wish for.

You have chosen to live in London and make a life there. Now I need you to look into your heart. If you decide that you wish for ownership of Il Boschetto di Sole then I need some indication that this wish is real—that you are willing to settle down. If you have no wish for this I would not burden you.

Whatever you decide, I wish you well in life.

Yours with affection,
Roberto Bianchi

The letter was so typical of Count Roberto that Holly could almost hear his baritone voice speaking the words. He wanted the land he loved to go to someone who held his own values and shared his vision. He knew her father did, but he didn't know if Holly did or not. In truth, she wasn't sure herself. But she also knew that in this case it didn't matter. Her father loved Il Boschetto di Sole—it was the land of his heart—and to own it would give him pure, sheer joy. She loved her father, and therefore she would fight for Il Boschetto di Sole with all her might.

Simple.

Holly clenched her hands into fists and stared at the door to await the return of the exiled Prince of Lycander.

CHAPTER TWO

STEFAN SEATED HIMSELF in the small annexe room and glared down at the letter, distaste already curdling inside him. The whole thing was reminiscent of the manipulative ploys and stratagems his father had favoured. Alphonse had delighted in the pulling of strings and the resultant antics of those whom he controlled.

During the custody battle he had stripped Eloise of everything—material possessions and every last vestige of dignity—and relished her humiliation. He had smeared her name, branded her a harlot and a tramp, an unfit mother and a gold-digger. All because he had held the trump card at every negotiation. He'd had physical possession of Stefan, and under Lycandrian law, as ruler, he had the final say in court. So, under threat of never seeing her son again, Eloise had accepted whatever terms Alphonse offered, all through her love for Stefan.

She had given up everything, allowed herself to be vilified simply in order to be granted an occasional visit with her son at Alphonse's whim.

In the end even those had been taken from her. Alphonse had decided that the visits 'weakened' his son, and that his attachment to his mother was 'bad' for him. That he could never be tough enough, princely enough, whilst he still saw his mother. So he had rescinded her visitation rights and cast Eloise from Lycander.

Once in London Eloise had suffered a breakdown, followed by a mercifully short but terminal illness.

Guilt twisted his insides anew—he had failed her.

Enough. He would not walk that bleak memory-lined road now. Because the past could not be changed. Right now he needed to read this letter and figure out what to do about this unexpected curveball.

Distasteful and manipulative it might be, but it was an opportunity to win possession of some important land in Lycander in his own right. The idea brought him a surge of satisfaction—his father had not prohibited him from *inheriting* land.

So this would allow him to return to Lycander on his terms. But it was more than that… The idea of owning a place his mother had loved touched him with a warmth he couldn't fully understand. Perhaps on Il Boschetto di Sole he could feel close to her again.

So all he needed to do was beat Holly Romano.

Holly Romano… Curiosity surfaced. The look she had cast him when she'd learned his identity had held more than a hint of animosity, and that had been before they'd heard the terms of the will. Perhaps she had simply suspected that they were destined to be cast as adversaries, but instinct told him it was more than that. There had been something personal in that look of deep dislike, and yet he was positive they had never met.

No way would he have forgotten. Her beauty was unquestionable—corn-blonde hair cascaded halfway down her back, eyes of cerulean blue shone under strong brows, and she had a retroussé nose, a generous mouth…and a body that Stefan suspected would haunt his dreams. *Whoa.* No need to go over the top. After all, he was no stranger to beautiful women—the combination of his royal status and his wealth made him a constant target for women on the catch, sure they could ensnare him into marriage.

Stefan had little or no compunction in disillusioning them.

Enough. Open the damn letter, Petrelli.

The handwriting was curved and loopy, but strong, Roberto Bianchi might have been ill but he had been firm of purpose.

Dear Stefan

I am sure you are surprised by the terms of my will. Let me explain.

Your mother was like a daughter to me. I was her godfather, and after her parents' death I became her guardian. As she grew up she spent a lot of her time at Il Boschetto di Sole and I believe she was happy there, on that beautiful, fragrant land.

It was a happiness that ceased very soon after her marriage to your father—a marriage I deeply regret I encouraged her to go through with.

In my—poor—defence I was dazzled by the idea of a royal alliance, and Alphonse could be charming when he chose. I believed he would care for your mother and that she would be able to do good as ruler of Lycander.

I also did not wish to encourage her relationship with Thomas Romano—a man of indifferent social status who was already engaged.

Stefan stopped reading as his mind assimilated that information. His mother and Thomas Romano had been an item. A pang of sorrow hit him. There was so much he didn't know about Eloise—so much he wished he could have had time to find out.

As you know, your parents' marriage was destined for disaster, and by the time I realised my mistake there was nothing I could do.

Your father forbade Eloise from seeing me, and not even my influence could change that. In the end he made it a part of the custody agreement that if Eloise saw me she would be denied even the very few visits she was allowed with you.

Stefan stopped reading as white-hot anger burned inside him. There had been no end to Alphonse's vindictiveness. Familiar guilt intensified within him. Eloise had given up so very much for him, and had had no redress in a court in a land where the ruler's word was law.

When Eloise left Lycander I was unable to find her—I promise you, I tried. I wish with all my heart she had contacted me—I believe and I hope she would have if illness hadn't overcome her.

If Eloise were alive I would leave Il Boschetto di Sole to her. Instead I have decided to give you, her son, a chance to own it. In this way I hope I can make up to you the wrong I did your mother. I want to give you the opportunity to return to Lycander as I believe your mother would have wished.

Eloise was happy at Il Boschetto di Sole, and I truly believe that if she is looking down it will give her peace to see you settled on the land she loved. Land you could pass on to your children, allowing the grove to continue as it has for generations—as an inde-

pendent business that passes from father and
mother to son or daughter.
    If you wish this, then I wish you luck.
    Yours sincerely,
    Roberto Bianchi

Stefan let the letter fall onto his knees as he considered its contents. He hadn't set foot in Lycander for eight years. The idea of a return to his birthplace was an impossibility unless he accepted his brother's charity. But now he had an opportunity to return under his own steam, to own land in his own right, defy his father's edict and win the place his mother had loved—a place she would have wanted him to have.

He closed his eyes and could almost see her, her delicate face framed with dark hair, her gentle smile.

But what about the Romano claim?

Not his concern—*he* hadn't made this will. Roberto Bianchi had decided that the grove should go either to Holly Romano or himself. So be it. This was his way back to Lycander and he would take it. But he was damned if he'd jump to Roberto Bianchi's tune.

* * *

Holly watched as Stefan re-entered the room, his stride full of purpose as he faced the lawyer.

'I'll need a copy of the will to be sent to my lawyers asap.'

James Simpson rose from behind his desk. 'Not a problem. Can I ask why?'

'Because I plan to overturn the terms of the will.'

The lawyer shook his head and a small smile touched his thin lips. 'With all due respect, you can try but you will not succeed. Roberto Bianchi was no fool and neither am I. You will not be able to do it.'

'That remains to be seen,' Stefan said, a stubborn tilt to the square of his jaw. 'But in the meantime perhaps it would be better for you to tell us any other provisions the Count saw fit to insert.'

'No matter what the outcome, Thomas Romano retains the right to live in the house he currently occupies until his death, and an amount of three times his current annual salary will be paid to him every year, regardless of his job status.'

Holly frowned. 'So in other words the new

owner can sack him but he will still have to pay him and he can keep his house?'

She could see that sounded fair enough, but she knew that her father would dwindle away if his job was taken from him—if he had to watch someone else manage Il Boschetto di Sole. Especially Stefan Petrelli—the son of the woman he had once loved, the woman who had rejected him and broken his heart.

'Correct.' James Simpson inclined his head. 'There are no other provisions.'

Stefan leant forward. 'In that case I would appreciate a chance to speak with Ms Romano in private.'

Suspicion sparked—perhaps Stefan Petrelli thought he could buy her off? But alongside her wariness was a flicker of anticipation at the idea of being alone with him. How stupid was *that*? Hard to believe her hormones hadn't caught up with the message—this man was the enemy. Although perhaps it didn't have to be like that. Perhaps she could persuade him to cede his claim. After all, he hadn't set foot in Lycander in years—why on earth did he even *want* Il Boschetto di Sole?

'Agreed.'

The lawyer inclined his head. 'There is a meeting room down the hall.'

Minutes later they were in a room full of gleaming chrome and glass, where modern art splashed bright white walls and vast windows overlooked the City and proclaimed that Simpson, Wright and Gallagher were undoubtedly prime players in the world of law.

'So,' Stefan said. 'This isn't what I was expecting when I woke up this morning.'

'That's an understatement.'

His gaze assessed her. 'Surely this can't be a surprise to you? You knew Roberto Bianchi, and it sounds like the Romanos have been an integral part of Il Boschetto di Sole for centuries.'

'Roberto Bianchi was a man who believed in duty above all else. I thought he would leave his estate intact. Turns out he couldn't bear the thought of the grove being sucked up by a corporation.'

'Why?'

Holly stared at him. He looked genuinely bemused. 'Because to Count Roberto Il Boschetto di Sole truly was a place of sunshine—he loved it, heart and soul. As my father does.' She gave a heartbeat of hesitation. 'As I do.'

Something flashed across his eyes—something she couldn't fathom. But whatever it was it hardened his expression.

'Yet you live and work in London?'

'How do you know where I work or live? Did you check me out?'

'I checked out your public profiles. That is the point of them—they are *public*.'

'Yes. But...' Though really there were no 'buts'—he was correct, and yet irrationally she was still outraged.

'I did a basic social media search—you work for Lamberts Marketing, as part of their admin team. That doesn't sound like someone whose heart and soul are linked to a lemon grove in Lycander.'

'It's temporary. I thought working for a marketing company for a short time would give me some useful insights and skills which will be transferrable to Il Boschetto di Sole. My plan is to return in six months.'

Yes, she loved London, but she had always known it was a short-term stay. Her father would be devastated if she decided not to return to Lycander, to her life on Il Boschetto di Sole. She was a Romano, and that was where she belonged. Of course he wouldn't force her return—but he needed her.

Ever since her mother had left Holly had vowed she would look after him—especially since he'd been diagnosed with a long-term heart condition. There was no immediate danger, and provided he looked after himself he should be fine. But that wasn't his forte. He was a workaholic and the extent of his cooking ability was to dial for a take away.

Guilt panged anew—she shouldn't have left in the first place. The least she could have done for the man who had brought her up singlehandedly from the age of eight was not abandon him. But she visited regularly, checked up nearly daily, and she would be home soon.

Stefan stepped a little closer to her—not into her space, but close enough that for a stupid moment she caught a whiff of his scent, a citrus woodsy smell that sent her absurdly dizzy.

For a second his body tensed, and she would have sworn he caught his breath, and then he frowned—as though he'd lost track of the conversational thread just as she had.

Focus.

'I'd like to discuss a deal,' he said eventually, as the frown deepened into what she was coming to think of as his trademark scowl. 'What will it take for you to walk away from this? I understand that you are worried about your father—but I would guarantee that his job is safe, that nothing will change for him. If anything, he would have more autonomy to do as he wishes with the grove. And you can name your price—what do you want?'

Holly's eyes narrowed. 'I don't want anything.'

'You don't even want to think about it?' Disbelief tinged each syllable.

'Nope.'

'Why not?' The question was genuine, but lined with an edge—this was a man used to getting his own way.

'Because the Romanos have toiled on that land for generations—now we have a chance to own the land in our own right. Nothing is worth more than that. *Nothing.* Surely you see that?'

'No, I don't. It is just soil and fruit and land—

the same as any other on Lycander. Take the money and buy another lemon grove—a new one that can belong to the Romanos from the start.'

His tone implied that he genuinely believed this to be a viable solution. 'It doesn't work like that. We have a history with Il Boschetto di Sole—a connection, a bond. *You* don't.'

His frown deepened but he remained silent; it was impossible to tell his thoughts.

'So why don't you take your own advice? You have more than enough money to buy a score of lemon groves. Why do you want *this* one?'

'That's my business,' he said. 'The point is I am willing to pay you well over the market price. I suggest you think carefully about my offer. Because I am also willing to fight it out, and if I win then you will have nothing. No money and no guarantee that your father will keep his job.'

For a second her blood chilled and anger soared. 'So if you win you would take his job from him?'

'Perhaps. If I win the grove it will be mine to do with as I wish.'

For a second a small doubt trickled through her—what if she lost and was left with nothing? But this wasn't about money; this was about the land of her father's heart. This was her opportunity to give her father something infinitely precious, and she had no intention of rolling over and conceding.

'No deal. If you want a fight, bring it on. This meeting is over.'

Before she could head around the immense table he moved to intercept her. 'Where are you going? To marry the first man you find?'

'Perhaps I am. Or perhaps I already have a boyfriend ready and eager to walk me to the altar.'

As if. Post-Graham she had decided to eschew boyfriends and to run away screaming from any altar in sight.

'Equally, I'm sure there will be women queuing round the block to marry *you*.'

He gusted out a sigh, looking less than enamoured at the thought. 'For a start, I'm pretty sure it's not that easy to just get married—there will be plenty of red tape and bureaucracy to get through. Secondly, I have a better idea than instant matrimony, even if it were possible. Let's call a truce on the race to the altar whilst my lawyers look at the will and see if this whole marriage stipulation can be overturned. There has to be a better way to settle this.'

'No argument here—that makes sense.' Caution kicked in. 'In theory...' Because it could be a trick—why should she believe anything Stefan Petrelli said? 'But what's to stop you from marrying someone during our 'truce' as a back-up plan?'

Call her cynical, but she had little doubt that a millionaire prince could find a way to obliterate all red tape and bureaucracy.

'The fact that even the thought of marriage makes me come out in hives.'

'Hives may be a worthwhile price to pay for Il Boschetto di Sole.'

'Point taken. In truth there is nothing to stop either of us reneging on a truce—and it would be foolish for either of us to trust the other.' Rubbing the back of his neck, he looked at her. 'The lawyers will work fast—that's what I pay them for. We're probably only talking twenty-four hours—two days, tops. We'll need to stick together until they get back to us.'

Stick together. The words resonated in the echoey confines of the meeting room, pinged into the sudden silence, bounced off the chrome and glass and writhed into images that brought heat to her cheeks.

Something sparked in his grey eyes, calling to her to close the gap between them and plaster herself to his chest.

'No way.' The words fell from her lips with vehemence, though whether it was directed at herself or him she wasn't sure.

In truth, he looked a little poleaxed himself, and in that instant Holly wondered if this attraction could be mutual.

Then, as if with an effort, he shrugged. 'What's the alternative? Seems to me it's a good idea to spend one weekend together in the hope that we can avoid a year of marriage.'

Deep breath, Holly. His words held reason, and no way would she actually succumb to this insane attraction—she'd steered clear of the opposite sex for eighteen months now, without regret. Yet the whole idea of sticking to Stefan Petrelli caused her lungs to constrict. *Go figure.*

'How would it work?'

'I suggest a hotel. Neutral ground. We can get a suite. Two bedrooms and a living area.'

Had there been undue emphasis on the word 'two'? A glance at his expression showed tension in his jaw—clearly he wasn't overly keen on the logistics of them sticking together either. But she couldn't come up with an alternative—couldn't risk him heading to the altar, and definitely couldn't trust him. And this was doable. A suite. Separate bedrooms.

So... 'That could work.'

'What are your plans for the weekend? We can do our best to incorporate them.'

'Nothing I can't reschedule.'

In fact her plans had been to work, chill out and continue her exploration of London—maybe meet up with a colleague for a quick drink or to catch a film. But such a programme made her sound like a complete Billy-no-mates. In truth she had kept herself to herself in London, because she'd figured there was no point getting too settled in a life she knew to be strictly temporary.

'I do have some work to do, but I can do that anywhere with internet. What about you?'

'I've got some meetings, but like you I should be able to reschedule. Though I do have one site visit I can't postpone. I suggest we go there first, then find a hotel and swing by our respective houses for some clothes.'

'Works for me.'

It would all be fine.

One weekend—how hard could it be?

CHAPTER THREE

STEFAN FIDGETED IN the incredibly comfortable Tudor-style seat that blended into the discreetly lavish décor of the Knightsbridge hotel. Gold fabrics adorned the lounge furniture, contrasting with the deep red of the thick curtains, and the walls were hung with paintings that depicted the Tudor era—Henry VIII in all his glory, surrounded by miniatures of all his wives.

The irony was not lost on Stefan—his own father was reminiscent of that monarch of centuries ago. Cruel, greedy, and with a propensity to get through wives. Alphonse's tally had been four.

Stefan tugged his gaze from the jewelled pomp of Henry, fidgeted again, drummed his fingers on the ornamental desk, then realised he was doing so and gritted his teeth. What was *wrong* with him?

Don't kid yourself.

He'd already identified the problem—he was

distracted by the sheer proximity of Holly Romano. Had been all day. To be fair, it wasn't her fault. Earlier, at his suggestion, she'd remained in the car whilst he conducted the site visit; now they were in the hotel and for the most part she was absorbed in her work. Her focus on the computer screen nearly absolute.

Nearly.

But every so often her gaze flickered to him and he'd hear a small intake of breath, glimpse the crossing and uncrossing of long, slender jean-clad legs and he'd know that Holly was every bit as aware of him as he was of her.

Dammit!

Attraction—mutual or otherwise—had no place here. Misplaced allure could *not* muddy the waters. He wanted Il Boschetto di Sole.

An afternoon of fact-finding had elicited the news that the lemon grove wasn't just lucrative—a fact that meant nothing to him—but was also strategically important. Its produce was renowned. It generated a significant amount of employment and a large chunk of tax revenue for the crown.

Ownership of Il Boschetto di Sole would bring

him influence in Lycander—give him back something that his father had taken from him and that his brother would grant only as a favour. For it to come from a place his mother had loved would add a poignancy that mattered more than he wanted to acknowledge. Perhaps there he could feel closer to her—less guilty, less tormented by the memory of his betrayal.

He could even move her urn of ashes from the anonymous London cemetery where her funeral service had taken place. For years he had done his best, made regular pilgrimage, laid flowers. He had had an expensive plaque made, donated money for a remembrance garden. But if he owned the grove he would be able to scatter her ashes in a place she had loved, a place where she could be at peace.

His gaze drifted to Holly Romano again. He wanted to come to a fair deal with her, despite her vehement repudiation of the idea. His father had never cared about fairness, simply about winning, crushing his opponent—Stefan had vowed never to be like that. Any deal he made would be a fair one. Yes, he'd win, but he'd do it fair and square and where possible he'd treat his adversary with respect.

He pushed thoughts of Alphonse from his mind, allowed himself instead to study Holly's face. There was a small wrinkle to her brow as she surveyed the screen in front of her, her blonde head tilted to one side, the glorious curtain of golden hair piled over one shoulder. Every so often she'd raise her hand to push a tendril behind her ear, only for it to fall loose once more. There came that insidious tug of desire again— one he needed to dampen down.

As if sensing his scrutiny, she looked up.

Good one, Petrelli. Caught staring like an adolescent. 'Just wondering what you're working on. Admin isn't usually so absorbing.'

There was a hesitation, and then she spun the screen round to show him. 'It's no big deal. One of the managers at work has offered to mentor me and she's given me an assignment.' She gave a hitch of her slender shoulders. 'It's just some research—no big deal.'

Only clearly it was—the repetition, her failed attempt to appear casual indicated that.

'Maybe you should consider asking to move out of admin and into a marketing role.'

'No point. I'm going back home in a few months.'

Then why bother to be mentored? he wondered.

As if in answer to his unspoken question she turned to face him, her arms folded. 'I want to learn as much as I can whilst I'm here, to maximise how I can help when I get back.'

It made sense, and yet he intuited it was more than that. Perhaps he should file it away as potentially useful information. Perhaps he should make a push to find something he could bring to the negotiating table.

'Fair enough.' A glance outside showed the autumn dusk had settled in, which meant... 'I'm ready for dinner—what about you?'

'Um... I didn't realise it was so late. I'm quite happy to grab a sandwich in my room. I bet Room Service is pretty spectacular here.'

'I'm sure it is, but I've heard the restaurant is incredible.'

Blue eyes surveyed him for a moment. 'So you're suggesting we go and have dinner together in the restaurant?'

'Sure. Why not? The reviews are fantastic.'

'And you're still hoping to convince me to cut a deal and cede my claim.'

'Yes.'

'It won't work.' There was steel in her voice.

'That doesn't mean I shouldn't try. Hell, don't you want to convince me to do the same?'

'Well, yes, but...'

'Then we may as well pitch over a Michelin-starred meal, don't you think?'

She chewed her bottom lip, blue eyes bright with suspicion, and then her tummy gave a less than discreet growl. She rolled her eyes, but her lips turned up in a sudden smile.

'See? Your stomach is voting with me.'

'Guess my brain is outvoted, then,' she muttered, and she rose from the chair. 'I'll be five minutes.'

True to her word she emerged just a few moments later. She'd changed back into the charcoal skirt she'd worn earlier, topped now by a crimson blouse. Her hair was swept up in an artlessly elegant arrangement, with tendrils free to frame her face.

In that moment he wished with a strangely

fierce yearn that this was a date—a casual, easy, get-to-know-you-dinner with the possibility of their attraction progressing. But it wasn't and it couldn't be. This was a fact-finding mission.

Suddenly his father's words echoed in his ears with a discordant buzz.

'Information is power, Stefan. Once you know what makes someone tick you can work out how to turn that tick to a tock.'

That was what he needed to focus on—gaining information. Not to penalise her but so that he could work out a fair deal.

Resolutely turning his gaze away from her, he made for the door. But as they headed down plush carpeted corridors and polished wooden stairs it was difficult to remain resolute. Somehow the glimpse of her hand as it slid down the gleaming oak banister, the elusive drift of her scent, the way she smoothed down her skirt all combined to add to the desire that tugged in his gut.

She paused on the threshold of the buzzing restaurant, a look of slight dismay on her face. 'I don't think I'm exactly dressed for this.'

'You look…' *Beautiful. Gorgeous.* Way better than any of the women sitting in white cushioned chairs braided with gold, around circular tables illuminated by candles atop them and chandeliers above. 'Fine,' he settled on.

Smooth, Petrelli, very smooth.

But oddly enough it seemed to do the trick. She looked up at him and a small smile tugged her lips upwards. 'Thank you. I know clothes shouldn't matter, but I am feeling a little inadequate in the designer department.'

'I'm hardly up to standard either,' he pointed out. 'I'm channelling the lumberjack look—the whole jeans and checked shirt image.'

The maître d' approached, a slightly pained expression on his face until he realised who Stefan was and his expression morphed to ingratiating. 'Mr Petrelli. This way, please.'

'People are wondering why we've been allowed in,' Holly whispered. 'They're all looking at us.'

'Let them look. In a minute George here will have discreetly spread the word as to who I am and that should do it. Royal entrepreneurial millionaire status transcends dress code. Especially when accompanied by a mystery guest.'

'Dressed from the High Street.' Her tone

sounded panicked. 'Oh, God. They won't call the press or anything, will they?'

'Not if they know what's good for them.'

She glanced over the menu at him. 'You don't like publicity, do you?'

In fact he loathed it—because no matter what he did, how many millions he'd made, whatever point he tried to get across, the press all wanted to talk about Lycander and he didn't. *Period.*

'Nope. So I think we're safe. Let's choose.'

After a moment of careful perusal he leant back.

'Hmm… What do you think? The duck sounds amazing—especially with the crushed pink peppercorns—but I'm not sure about adding cilantro in as well. But it could work. The starters look good too—though, again, I'm still not sure about fusion recipes.'

A small gurgle of laughter interrupted him and he glanced across at her.

'What?'

'I didn't have you down as a food buff. The lumberjack look didn't make me think gourmet.'

'I'm a man of many surprises.'

In truth, food was important to him—a result

of his childhood. Alphonse's toughening up regime had meant rationed food, and the clichéd bread and water diet had been a regular feature. His stomach panged in sudden memory of the gnaw of hunger, the doughy texture of the bread on his tongue as he tried to savour each nibble. He'd summoned up imaginary feasts, used his mind to conjure a cacophony of tastes and smells and textures. Vowed that one day he'd make those banquets real.

Whoa. Time to turn the memory tap off. Clearly his repressed memory banks had sprung a leak— one he intended to dam up right now.

The arrival of the waiter was a welcome distraction, and once they'd both ordered he focused on Holly. Her cerulean eyes were fringed by impossibly long dark lashes that contrasted with the corn-gold of her hair.

'And do you cook? Or just appreciate others' cooking?' she asked.

'I can cook, but I'm not an expert. When I have time I enjoy it. What about you?'

Holly grimaced. 'I can cook too, but I'm not inspired at all. I am a strict by-the-recipe girl. I wish I enjoyed it more, but I've always found it quite stressful.' Discomfort creased her forehead for a second, as if she regretted the words, and she looked down. 'Anyway, today I don't need to cook.'

For a stupid moment he wanted to probe, wanted to question the reason for that sudden flitting of sadness across her face.

Focus on the goal here, Petrelli.

He leant forward. 'If you accept my offer of a deal you could eat out every day. You need never touch a saucepan again.'

'Nice try, but no thanks. I'll soldier on. Truly, Stefan, nothing you offer me can top the idea of presenting Il Boschetto di Sole to my father.'

'That's the plan?'

'Yup.'

'You'll sign it over lock, stock and barrel?'

'Yup.'

'But that's nuts. Why hand over control?' The very idea gave him a sense of queasiness.

'Because it's the right thing to do.'

'If Roberto Bianchi had wanted your father to have the grove he'd have left it to him.'

Something that looked remarkably like guilt crossed her face as she shook her head. 'My fa-

ther has given his life to Il Boschetto di Sole—I
could never ask him to work for me. I respect him
too much. If the Romanos are to own the grove
then it will be done properly. Traditionally.'

'Pah!' The noise he'd emitted hopefully conveyed his feelings. 'Tradition? You will hand over
control because of *tradition*?'

'What is so wrong with that? Just because you
have decided to turn your back on tradition it
doesn't mean that's the right thing to do.'

His turn to hide the physical impact he felt at
her words—at the knowledge that Holly, like the
rest of Lycander, had judged him and found him
wanting.

No doubt she believed the propaganda and lies
Alphonse had spread and Stefan hadn't refuted.
Because in truth he'd welcomed it all. To him it
had put him in the same camp as his mother, had
made the guilt at his failure a little less.

'So you believe that just because something is
traditional it is right?'

'I didn't say that. But I believe history and tradition are important.'

'History is a great thing to learn from, but it
doesn't have to be repeated. It is progress that is

important—and if you don't change you can't progress. What if the inventor of the wheel had decided not to bother because *traditionally* people travelled by foot or on horseback? What about appalling traditions like slavery?'

'So do you believe monarchy is an appalling or outdated tradition? Do you believe Lycander should be a democracy?'

'I believe that is a debatable point. I do not believe that just because there has been a monarch for centuries there needs to be one for the next century. My point is that if the crown headed my way I would refuse it. Not on democratic principles but for personal reasons. I don't want to rule and I wouldn't change my whole life for the sake of tradition. Or duty.'

'So if Frederick had decided not to take the throne you would have refused it?'

'Yup.'

Stefan had no doubt of that. In truth he'd been surprised that Frederick had agreed. Their older half-brother Axel, Lycander's 'Golden Prince', had been destined to rule, and from all accounts would have made a great ruler.

As a child Stefan hadn't known Axel well—

he had been at boarding school, a distant figure, though he had always shown Stefan kindness when he'd seen him. Enough so that when Axel had died in a tragic car accident Stefan had felt grief and would have attended the funeral if his father had let him. But Alphonse had refused to allow Stefan to set foot on Lycandrian soil.

Axel's death had left Frederick next in line and his brother had stepped up. *More fool him.*

'My younger brothers would be welcome to it.'

'You'd have handed over the Lycandrian crown to one of the "Truly Terrible Twins"?'

An image of his half-brothers splashed on the front page of the tabloids crossed his mind. Emerson and Barrett rarely set foot in Lycander, but their exploits sold any number of scurrilous rags.

'Yes,' he stated—though even he could hear that his voice lacked total conviction.

Holly surveyed him through narrowed eyes. 'Forget tradition. What about duty? Wouldn't you have felt a *duty* to rule? A duty to your country?'

'Nope. I think Frederick's a first-class nutcase to take it on. I have one life, Holly, and I intend to live it for myself.' Exactly as he so wished his mother had done. 'I don't see anything wrong with that as long as I don't hurt anyone.'

She leaned across the table and her blue eyes sparkled, her face animated by the discourse. 'You could argue that by not taking the throne Frederick would have been hurting a whole country.'

Stefan surveyed her across the table and she nodded for emphasis, her lips parted in a small 'hah' of triumph at the point she'd made, and his gaze snagged on her mouth. Hard to remember the last time a date had sparked this level of discussion, had been happy to flat-out contradict him. Not that Holly *was* a date...

As the silence stretched a fraction too long her lips tipped in a small smirk. 'No answer to that?'

'Actually, I do. I just got distracted.'

For a moment confusion replaced the smirk. 'By wh—?' And then she realised, and a small flush climbed her cheekbones.

Now the silence shimmered. Her eyes dropped, skimmed over his chest, and then she rallied.

'Good excuse, Mr Petrelli, but I'm not buying it. You have no answer.'

For a moment he couldn't even remember the

question. *Think. They had been talking about Frederick.* What might have happened if he had refused the throne…

'I have an answer. It could be that Emerson or Barrett would turn into a great ruler. Or Lycander would become a successful democracy.'

'And you would be fine with that?'

'Sure. It doesn't mean I don't care about Lycander—I'm just not willing to give up my whole life for it, for the sake of tradition or because I "should". One life. One chance.'

His mother's life had been so short, so tragic, because of the decisions she'd made—decisions triggered by duty and love.

'Don't you agree?'

'No. Sometimes you have to do what you "should" do because it is the *right* thing to do. And that is more important than what you *want* to do.'

Stefan frowned, suspecting that she was speaking in specific terms rather than general. 'So what are your dreams? Your plans for life. Let's say you win Il Boschetto di Sole and give it to your father—what then?'

'Then I will help him—work the land, have

kids…' Her voice was even; the animation had vanished.

'And if you don't win?'

'I *will* win.'

He raised an eyebrow. 'Humour me. It's a hypothetical question.'

'I don't know… I would have to see what my father wished to do—whether he wanted to stay on at Il Boschetto di Sole, what your plans for the grove would be.'

'OK. So let's say your father decides to retire, live out the rest of his life peacefully in his home or elsewhere in Lycander.' A memory of her utter focus on her work earlier came to him. 'What about marketing? Would you like to give that a go? Build a career?'

There was a flash in her blue eyes; he blinked and it was gone.

'My career is on Il Boschetto di Sole.'

'What is your job there?'

'I've helped out with most things, but I was working in admin before…before I came to London.'

'Tell me about what you were working on earlier today. In the suite.'

A hesitation and then a shrug. A pause as the waiter arrived with their starters. She thanked him, speared a king prawn and then started to speak.

'Lamberts have a pretty major client in the publishing field and they're looking to rebrand their crime line. I've been working on that.'

Her voice started out matter-of-fact, but as she talked her features lit up and her gestures were expressive of the sheer enthusiasm the project had ignited in her.

'I've helped put a survey together—you know, a sort of list of twenty questions about what makes a reader choose a new book or author, what sort of cover would inspire them to give something a try... Blood and gore versus a good-looking protagonist. Also, do people prefer series or stand-alones? We'll need to analyse all the data and come up with some options and then get reader opinion across a broad spectrum. Because we also want to attract readers who don't usually read that genre. Then we need some social media, some—'

She broke off.

'Oh, God. How long have I been talking for?

You should have stopped me before you went co-
matose with boredom.'

'Impossible.'

'To stop me?'

Her stricken look made him smile. 'No! I meant
it would have been impossible for me to have
been bored. When you speak of this project you
light up with sheer passion.'

The word caused him to pause, conjuring up
other types of passion, and he wondered if her
thoughts had gone the same way.

Unable to stop himself, he reached out, gently
stroked her cheek. 'You are flushed with enthusiasm...your eyes are alight, your whole body is
engaged.'

Stop right there. Move your hand away.

Yet that was nigh on impossible. The softness
of her skin, her small gasp, the way her teeth had
caught her under lip as her eyes widened... All
he wanted to do was kiss her.

Cool it, Petrelli.

Failing finding a handy waiter with an ice
bucket, he was going to have to find some inner
ice.

Leaning back, he forced his voice into objective mode. 'Sounds to me as though what you want to do is pursue a career in marketing. Not take up a job on Il Boschetto di Sole.'

She blinked, as if his words had broken a spell, and her lips pressed together and her eyes narrowed as she shook her head. Shook it hard enough that tendrils of hair fell loose from her strategically messy bun.

'That is not for me. I couldn't do what you did. Walk away from my duty to pursue a career.'

Her words served as effectively as an ice bucket could have and he couldn't hold back an instinctive sound of denial. 'That's not exactly how it went down.'

'So how *did* it go down? As I remember it, you decided to renounce Lycander and your royal duties to live your own life—away from a country you felt you had no allegiance to. But you were happy to accept a severance hand-out from Alphonse to help set you up in the property business.'

Gall twisted his insides that she should believe that.

'Alphonse gave me nothing.'

And Stefan wouldn't have taken it if he had tried.

'I ended up in property because it was the only job I could find.'

He could still taste the bitter tang of grief, fear and desperation. He'd arrived in London buoyed up by a sense of freedom and relief that he'd finally escaped his father, determined to find out what had happened to his mother. His discoveries had caused a cold anger to burn inside him alongside a raging inferno of guilt.

His mother had suffered a serious mental breakdown. The staff at the hostel that had taken her in had had no idea of her identity, but to Stefan's eternal gratitude they had looked after her. Though Eloise had never really recovered, relapsing and lurching from periods of depression to episodes of relative calm until illness had overtaken her.

In his anger and grief he had started his search for a job under an assumed name, changed his surname by deed poll and got himself new documentation, determined to prove himself without any reference to his royal status.

It hadn't been easy. And he would be grateful

for ever to the small independent estate agent who'd taken pity on him. His need for commission had honed his hitherto non-existent sales skills and negotiating had come naturally to him.

'Luckily I was a natural and it piqued my interest.'

Holly tipped her head to one side. 'But how did you go from that job to a multibillion-pound business?'

Was that suspicion in her voice? The idea that she still believed Alphonse had funded him shouldn't matter but it did.

'I worked hard and I saved hard. I worked multiple jobs, I persuaded a bank to take a chance on me, I studied the market and invested in properties until I had a diverse portfolio. Some properties I bought, did up and sold, others I rented out. Once my portfolio became big enough I set up a company. It all spiralled from there.'

And when it had he had resumed his own identity, wanting the world to know what he had made of himself.

'You make it sound easy.'

'It wasn't. Point is, though, I did it on my own.'

Holly was silent for a moment, almost absentmindedly forking up some Udon noodles. 'So what about today? That site we visited? It looked like it was in a pretty poor area.'

'It is. We're building social housing. Projects like that are taken on by a separate arm of my business. The problem with the housing market is the huge differential in regional properties, and overall houses are becoming unaffordable—which is wrong. Equally, there is insufficient social housing and the system can backfire, or people are expected to live in unsafe, horrible conditions and not have a lot of redress. I work to try and prevent that. I plough a proportion of the company's profits back into building more houses, better houses. More affordable houses. Both for young people to buy and people who can't afford to buy to rent at reasonable prices. And for those who haven't the money to afford the most basic of rent. The amount of homeless-ness in rich countries is criminal and—'

He broke off.

'Sorry. It's a bit of a pet peeve I have. No need to bore you with it.' But it was a subject that he felt strongly about. His mother had spent periods of time homeless, too ill after her breakdown to figure out the benefits system.

'I'm not bored either,' Holly said softly. 'I think your commitment to put money into the system, to help people, is fantastic. Your enthusiasm lights up your face.'

She lifted her hand in a mirror gesture of his earlier one and touched his cheek, and his heart pounded his ribcage.

'I admire that. As well as your phenomenal success. I feel bad that I believed Alphonse funded it.'

'It's OK.' He knew the whole of Lycander believed the same; his father's propaganda machine had churned out fictional anti-Stefan stories with scurrilous precision.

'But why don't you set the record straight?'

Her hand dropped to cover his; she stroked her thumb across the back and his body stilled as desire pooled in his gut.

'There is no point. For a start, who would believe me? Plus, at the end of the day I did walk away from Lycander.'

'Then why do you want Il Boschetto di Sole? You own properties throughout Europe. Why do you want one Lycandrian lemon grove if you have no love for Lycander at all?'

An image of his birthplace suddenly hit him— the roll of verdant fields, the swoop and soar and dip of the hills, the spires and turrets of the architecture of the city, the scent of lemon and blossom and spices borne on a breeze…

Whoa. It was a beautiful place but he owed it nothing. Rather it was the other way round. His father had taken away what was rightfully his and this was a way to redress the balance. A way to take his mother's ashes to their final resting place. *That* was what was important. This visceral reaction to Holly needed to be doused, and this emotional conversation with its undertones of attraction needed to cease.

'I'm a businessman, Holly. Why would I pass up the chance to add this to my portfolio?'

Her hand flew from his as if burnt, and he realised the words had come out with a harshness he hadn't intended. But it didn't matter. He and Holly Romano were adversaries, not potential bed-mates.

Her eyes hardened, as if she had caught the same thought. 'Good question. And now, seeing as the point of this dinner is to pitch to each other, do you mind if I go first?'

Stefan nodded. 'Go ahead.'

CHAPTER FOUR

HOLLY WAITED AS their main courses arrived, smiling up at the waiter, relieved at the time-out as her mind and body struggled to come to terms with the conversation. Her cheek still tingled from his touch and her fingers still held the roughness of his five o'clock shadow, the strength and breadth of his hand under hers.

This whole dinner had been a mistake, but somehow she had to try and salvage it. Though she suspected it was a doomed pitch, because she had nothing to offer. The only thing she could sell was the moral high ground, launching an appeal to his better, altruistic self. And whilst he clearly *had* one she didn't think it would come to the table on this issue.

So here went nothing.

'I understand you don't believe in tradition, but I hope you believe in fairness. I believe the Romano claim is stronger than yours. We have a true connection with Il Boschetto di Sole and we already fulfil one of Roberto Bianchi's wishes. For the grove to be a family affair, handed on from generation to generation.'

A pause showed her that he looked unmoved, his expression neutral as he listened.

'Also, you have no real financial incentive to pursue this—if you truly wish for land in Lycander you can afford to buy it. I know your father passed a law that made that difficult but surely your brother would rescind that decree?'

His dark eyebrows jerked upwards. 'And what do you base *that* opinion on? I didn't realise you had an inside track to the Crown Prince.'

A flush touched her cheek as she realised he was right; she had no idea of the relationship between the brothers but it obviously wasn't a close one.

'Are you saying he won't?'

'No. I am saying I don't wish to ask him.' His face was shuttered now, his lips set in a grim line, his eyes shadowed. 'This is my opportunity to own land in Lycander. Lucrative, strategic land— the equivalent to what I lost. You can't change my mind on this, I accept you have a case, but I'll fight you all the way.'

'Even if your lawyers can't find a loophole and you have to get married?' Perhaps she was clutching at straws, but she had to try. 'You said the thought of marriage makes you break out in hives. Imagine what actually going through with it would do to you? Surely you'd rather ask Frederick to grant you a land licence?'

Forget shutters. This time the metaphorical equivalent of a metal grille slammed down on his expression.

'Nope. If I have to get married for a year I'll suck it up.'

'But it's more complicated than that.'

'How so?'

'What about children?'

'What *about* them?'

Holly sighed. 'As I've already mentioned, Roberto Bianchi wanted Il Boschetto di Sole to pass from generation to generation—from father to son, or mother to daughter. That means that technically you'd need a son or daughter to pass it on to.'

He placed his fork down with a clatter. 'Without disrespect, Holly, Count Roberto is dead, and he certainly cannot dictate whether or not I choose to have children.'

'No, but surely you want to respect his wishes?'

'Why? I think the whole will is nuts—that's why I am trying to overturn it.'

'And I agree with that. But I don't think we can ignore what he wanted long-term. He truly *loved* Il Boschetto di Sole.'

'And I hope it brought him happiness in his lifetime. Now he is gone, and I will not alter my entire life to accommodate him. I certainly won't bring children into this world solely to be heir to a lemon grove. That would hardly be fair to them *or* me.'

She couldn't help but flinch, and hastily reached out for her wine glass in an attempt to cover it up. After all that was exactly why her parents had wanted a child so desperately—only they hadn't just wanted a child. They'd wanted a son.

His forehead creased in curiosity as he leaned over to top up her wine glass. 'Would you do it?'

'No. Not only for that!'

And yet she found her gaze skittering away from his. Her whole life her father had impressed upon her the importance of marriage and children, the need for a Romano heir to carry on tradition.

'Yes, I wanted to get married and have a family, but not only for the sake of Il Boschetto di Sole. I wanted it for *me.*'

The whole package: to love and be loved, to experience family life as it should be. With two loving parents offering unconditional love, untinged by disappointment.

One of those detestable eyebrows rose. '*Wanted?* Past tense?'

Holly speared a lightly roasted cherry tomato with unnecessary force. '*Want.* That is what I want.'

'So what happens if your children don't want to run a lemon grove? If they have other dreams or ambitions? What if they want to become a pilot or a doctor or a surfer?'

'Then of course they can.' And if he raised that bloody eyebrow again, so help her, she'd figure out a way to shave it off.

'But what about tradition and duty then? Surely if it's right for *you* to follow the path of duty it is right for them too?'

'I *want* to follow that path. I hope my children will want to as well, but if they don't I won't force them to.' Could she sound *any* lamer? Time to change tack. 'Anyway, at least I'll have a shot at fulfilling Roberto's wishes. Are you saying you have *no* plans to have children?'

'Got it in one. I have no intention of getting married if I can avoid it, or entering into any form of long-term relationship, and I won't risk my child being torn between two parents. It is as simple as that.'

His tone was flat, but for a second Holly had a glimpse of the younger Stefan, who had been torn between two parents. The custody battle, whilst one-sided, had been long and drawn-out, though the outcome had never been in doubt. An outcome that Alphonse had, of course, claimed to be better for Stefan—after all, Eloise had been condemned as an unfit mother, an unfaithful wife who had only married Alphonse for his money.

Holly had believed every word—after all, Eloise had already ruined her parents' marriage.

But... 'Some parents manage to negotiate a fair agreement.'

'That's not a risk I'm willing to take. I will not

bring a child into this world unless I can guarantee a happy childhood. As I can't, I won't.'

'You could opt for single parenthood. Adopt?'

He shook his head. 'Not for me. There are plenty of couples out there who want to adopt and can offer way more than I can. So, no. If the lawyers can't get us out of this I'll get married for a year. I'll do what it takes to win. Or my offer still stands. I'll buy you out here and now. You can start afresh—start a whole new Romano tradition if that's what floats your boat. That way you have a guaranteed win. Or you fight it out and risk ending up with nothing.'

The waiter returned, removed their empty plates and placed the dessert menu in front of them with discreet fluid movements, giving her a moment to let his deep chocolate tones run over her skin. Doubts swirled. Stefan Petrelli wanted Il Boschetto di Sole and she knew one way or another he would go all-out to get it.

She could end up with nothing. And yet... 'My father loves Il Boschetto di Sole—for him it would be unthinkable to give up the opportunity to own it.'

'What about you?'

Stefan held her gaze and she resisted the urge to wriggle on her seat.

'Is it unthinkable for you?'

Don't look away.

'Absolutely,' she stated.

There was no way she could let her father down over this—no way she could hand it over to Stefan. That was unthinkable.

So... 'No deal, Stefan. I too will fight and I will go all-out to win.'

'Then here's to a fair fight.'

The clink of glass against glass felt momentous, and then their mutual challenge seemed to swirl and change, morph into something else— an awareness and a mad, stupid urge to move around the table and kiss him.

Without meaning to she moistened her lips, and his grey eyes darkened with a veritable storm of desire.

Get a grip.

Yet she couldn't seem to break the spell. Any minute now she was going to do something inexplicably stupid.

Pushing her chair back with as much dignity as she could muster, she forced herself to smile.

'Just need the loo,' she said and, resisting the urge to run, she forced her feet to walk towards the door.

Stefan breathed out a deep breath he hadn't even been aware he'd been holding and tried to ignore the fact that his pulse-rate seemed to have upped a notch or three. This reaction to Holly was nuts. All he could hope was that his lawyers came through soon and this enforced proximity would come to a close.

Goodness only knew what it was about her... Yes, she was stunning, but it was more than that. There was something vulnerable about her, and that was exactly why he should be extra-wary. Thanks to the will Holly was on the opposite side of enemy lines, so any knight in shining armour urge needed to be tamped down. In truth, vulnerability did not usually appeal to him; he was no knight and well he knew it.

He took a few surreptitious deep breaths and kept his expression neutral as she walked back to the table, sat down and took up her knife and fork almost as if they were weaponry.

'So,' she said. 'Now the plan is to fight it out what happens next?'

'The truce holds until my lawyers call and then, depending on what they say, all bets are off. No loophole and we race to the nearest altar with whoever will marry us. If there *is* a loophole we fight it out in the courts.'

His mind whirred, looking for another option, because in truth neither of those appealed.

'Hard to know what to wish for.'

'The no marriage option has my vote.'

'But if it ends up in the courts it will come down to who has a better case. And how on earth can any judge decide that? It could drag on for years, and if it does Il Boschetto di Sole will end up with Crown Prince Frederick by default.'

Stefan's mouth hardened; there was no way on this earth he would let that happen.

He looked at her. 'So you'd prefer to duel it out through marriage?'

'I wouldn't call it a preference, exactly.' Her expression was suddenly unreadable. 'But maybe it would be easier?'

Stefan shook his head. 'It would be an equally big mess. For starters, let's say I find a bride before you find a groom. That still doesn't mean I win. I have to stay married for a year. What do I do if six months in she decides to divorce me, or threatens to divorce me?'

Not happening. He would not put himself in anyone's power. Ever again. As a child he'd been in his father's control. As an adult he controlled his own life, and the best way to maintain that control was not to cede it to anyone else. Physically or emotionally.

'Hmm…' She took a contemplative sip of wine, rubbed the tip of her nose in consideration. 'Or I could marry someone and stay married. Then I win and *then* he divorces me and demands half of Il Boschetto di Sole.'

Stefan watched her brooding expression and had a funny feeling she wasn't talking about a mythical person here.

'Or, even worse,' he offered, 'what if I marry someone and at the end of the year she wants to stay married and refuses to divorce me?'

Holly considered that for a moment and narrowed her eyes. 'What if it happens the other way round? She wants a divorce and you want to stay married?'

'Not happening.' Not on any planet, in any universe.

'Arrogant, much?'

'It's not arrogance. Most women in my experience are keen on the starry-eyed, happy-ever-after scenario. They must be overwhelmed by my good looks and rugged charm. Or could it be my bank balance and royal status?'

'Cynical, much?'

'Realistic, plenty.' Not one of the women he'd been with in the past years had been unaffected by his status.

'And that doesn't bother you?' Curiosity tinged her voice. 'That women want to be with you because of your assets—?' She broke off, a tinge of pink climbing her cheekbones as he raised his brows. 'Your *material* assets is what I meant. It *must* bother you.'

'Why? It makes it easier; we both make our terms clear at the outset. I always explain there will be no wedding bells ringing, that any relationship has no long-term future but I am happy to be generous in the interim and hopefully we'll have fun.'

'So, to sum you up: Stefan Petrelli—excellent

taste but short shelf-life and no long-term nour-ishment.'

'I can see why you're in marketing.' A sudden need to defend his position overcame him. 'I've had no complaints so far. I'm upfront, and I'm excellent boyfriend material. In fact next time I'm in the market for a girlfriend I'll give you a call to represent me.'

'No can do. I'm not sure I approve of the product.'

'Ha-ha!' Though he was pretty sure she wasn't joking.

She tipped her head to one side. 'So at the beginning of a relationship you tell a woman there can be no future in it but they all date you anyway?' Her tone indicated pure bafflement.

'Not all. Some women decline to take it beyond the first date, and I'm good with that. Others are happy with what's on offer.'

'So for you every relationship is a deal?'

'Yes. That makes sense to me.' And he wasn't about to apologise for it. 'There's no point starting a relationship if you both want completely different things. That's a sure-fire path to hurt and angst.'

A shadow crossed her face. 'Maybe you're right.' A quick shake of her head and she pushed her plate away, rested her elbows on the table and propped her chin in her hands. She watched him with evident fascination. 'So then what happens? You both set out your terms and then what?'

Aware of a slight sense of defensiveness, he continued. 'We go on another date and take things from there...'

'Take things *where*? If you both know there's no future, there is no destination.'

'That doesn't mean we can't enjoy the journey. Because it's not the future that is important. It's the here and now.'

Stefan had spent all his childhood focused on the future because his present had sucked. It had then turned out that the future he'd pictured hadn't panned out either. So now he figured it was all about optimising the present.

'If you spend all your time homing in on the future you never actually enjoy the here and now.'

'So if the two of you keep on enjoying the "here and now", why curtail that enjoyment? You may as well keep going on into the future.'

'Never happened. I guess I like variety.' Even

he cringed as he said it, but better to see the distaste that glinted in her eyes than pretend anything different. 'And so do the women I spend time with. I do my best to get involved with women with the same outlook as me. For the record, sometimes *she* ends it first—she opts to move on. Maybe to someone who has an interest in being seen, making headlines. Someone who wants to take extended holidays in the latest celeb hotspot.'

'So essentially you use each other and then trade in for a different model?'

'It works for me.'

He would never risk the idea that a woman's expectations might change, so it was always better to end it early so no one got hurt.

'On your terms?'

'On *agreed* terms. All we want is a good physical connection and some conversational sparkle over the dinner table every so often.'

'Define "every so often".'

'Once a week…once a fortnight. Depends on work commitments—hers and mine.'

There was a moment of silence—an instant during which Holly's eyes widened and looked almost dreamy, as if she were contemplating the whole idea. His heart-rate quickened and once again a wish that this *was* a date, that this conversation wasn't theoretical, pulsed through him. The urge to reach out, to take her hand, pull her up from the table and take her upstairs nearly overwhelmed him, and as her gaze met his he could feel his legs tense to propel him off his seat.

Whoa. Easy, Petrelli.

He didn't even know what her relationship criteria were. Whilst he'd been leaking information like a sieve he had no idea of *her* status.

'So what about you?'

'What *about* me?'

'What's your relationship slogan?'

'Holly Romano: uninterested, unavailable and un… something else. I'm on a relationship break.'

'Why?'

'Complicated break-up.'

He had the feeling she'd used that line before, perhaps to deflect unwanted attention, and the shadows in her eyes showed the truth of her words. Bleak shadows, like storm clouds on a summer's day. And there was a slump to her shoulders that betokened weariness. Only for an

instant, though, and then her body straightened
and she met his gaze.

'But if your lawyers don't find a loophole I'll
get over it. *Fast*. Because, like it or not, we'll both
have to contemplate matrimony. With or without romance.'

Picking up the bottle of wine, he topped up
their glasses. 'Yes, we will.'

A germ of an idea niggled at the back of his
brain, but before he could grasp it his phone
buzzed. A glance down showed his lawyer's
name. He looked around the still crowded restaurant and picked up.

'John. I'll call you back in five.'

Holly's eyes looked a question.

'Lawyer.' He rose to his feet. 'Guess we'll have
to skip dessert. I'd rather talk to him in private,
so let's head upstairs.'

CHAPTER FIVE

ONCE IN THE lounge area of their suite, Holly perched on the edge of a brocaded chair and watched as Stefan pulled his phone out of his pocket and pushed a button. Nerves sashayed through her as he paced the room with lithe strides. But her edginess wasn't only down to trepidation about his lawyer's verdict; her whole body was in a tizz.

There had been a moment—hell, way too many moments—over dinner, when she'd wanted nothing more than to be like one of the women he'd described. A woman happy to pursue the here and now and take advantage of the promise of a physical connection with him.

Ridiculous. And of all the men for her hormones to zone in on Stefan Petrelli was the most unsuitable—on a plethora of levels. She focused on the conversation.

'It's Stefan.'

He listened for a moment and his expression clouded, lips set in a line.

'You're sure?'

Another moment and he hung up, dropped the phone in his pocket and turned to face her.

Holly leant forward. 'There's no loophole, is there?'

'Not even a pinhead-sized one. James Simpson did a sterling job.'

'So we'll have to get married. Undertake that race to the altar.'

Holly clenched her hands as realisation washed over her. What an idiot she'd been. Instead of dining with Stefan Petrelli, getting her knickers in a knot over a Michelin-starred meal, she should have been shut up her room formulating a back-up plan. A marriage plan.

Chill.

It wasn't as if Stefan had been out there searching for a bride. That was the whole point of them staying together this weekend.

'Yes.'

The tightness of the syllable, the drumming of his fingers on his thigh, the increased speed of his stride all conveyed his dissatisfaction with the idea.

Holly got to her feet. 'Right. I'd better get going, then. The truce is over. The stick-together phase is finished.'

Yet her feet seemed reluctant to move—or rather, for reasons she couldn't fathom, they wanted to move towards Stefan rather than away. *Get a grip.* Talk about getting it wrong. Stefan was now officially the enemy.

'So I guess this is it.'

There was no guesswork involved. This was over. Next time she saw Stefan it would be in a court of law, once one of them had succeeded in marrying. So this was their last few minutes together.

Get a grip faster, Holly.

She'd only met the man this morning. What did she want? A greeting card moment?

Damn it. She knew exactly what she wanted and this was her only chance to get it.

Without allowing common sense to intervene, she let her hormones propel her forward. She was so close to him now that the merest sliver of air separated them. His scent assailed her, her whole body tingled, and her tummy felt weighted with a pool of heat. The scowl had vanished from his expression and his grey eyes gleamed in the moonlight. Molten desire sparked in their depths as he closed the tiny gap between them.

'I know this is mad,' she whispered. 'But as we won't be seeing each other again would you mind...kissing me?'

'Not a problem,' he growled instantly.

Sweet Lord—she couldn't have imagined a kiss such as this. His lips were firm, and she could taste a tang of wine, a hint of lemon... And then nothing mattered except the vortex of sheer sensation that flooded her every sense.

Desire mounted, and her calf muscles stretched as she went on tiptoe and twined her arms around his neck to pull him closer, pressed her body against his in a delicious wriggle of pleasure. She heard his groan, felt the heat of his large hands against the small of her back.

It was a kiss that might have gone on for ever, but eventually he gently pulled away. For a moment she stood, swayed, the only sound the mingle of their ragged breathing. Slowly reality intruded—the red and gold décor, the darkness outside illuminated by the London streetlights and the brightness of the moon.

Think. Speak. Move.

The directions seemed to be blocked. Her synapses were clearly misfiring…all signals from her brain were fuzzed by the aftershock of the kiss.

Do something.

Finally the order made its way through and she took a shaky step backwards, regained control of her vocal cords. 'Right. I'll be on my way, then.'

'No. Wait.'

To her irritation he had pulled himself together way faster than she had and now stood there eyeing her with a gleam of something she couldn't interpret.

'There is no need for me to wait.' To her relief, annoyance had served to dispel the effect of their lip-lock. 'I *need* to go and locate a groom.'

'Do you have anyone in mind?'

There was an edge to his voice. His grey eyes held a speculative nuance and she wondered if he was trying to probe her for information in the hope of using it against her.

'I have options,' she said, and kept her voice non-committal even as she reviewed said options.

Her father had suggested he speak with one of the Il Boschetto di Sole employees, but the idea left Holly cold. Graham still worked on the grove—and the thought of marrying *another* Il Boschetto di Sole employee, even in name only, felt foolhardy. An employee might well hold out hopes of becoming a co-owner, of remaining married to her. Come to that, *anyone* she married might think the same.

She ran her London colleagues through her mind—whittled them down to three possibilities. But she could hardly call them up and propose. Plus, she barely knew them—how could she trust any of them to stick to an agreement? Il Boschetto di Sole was a huge asset—an immensely lucrative business.

'But no one specific?' he persisted.

'I'm not a fool. I wouldn't tell you if I had. Do *you* have a bride lined up?'

Now his lips quirked up in a smile that left her both baffled and suspicious. 'I'm not sure. Let's just say I have an idea.'

Which put him ahead of the game—seeing as

his tone indicated that *his* idea was a good one and hers sucked. 'Bully for you. Now, I really need to go.'

'Give me five minutes. I need to make a phone call to my lawyers. I may have a way out of this. Promise me you won't go until I've talked to them.'

Holly hesitated. 'A way out that your hotshot lawyers haven't already thought of?'

'They don't call me The Negotiator for nothing.'

'I didn't know they called you The Negotiator at all.'

'I'll be five minutes. Tops.'

'OK. I'll pack slowly.'

In fact he was marginally longer than the allotted time, and she had her suitcase packed and was at the door before he emerged from his bedroom. To her irritation her tummy did a little flip-flop—he looked gorgeous, and his smile held a vestige of triumph as he walked towards her and gestured to the sofa.

'You may want to sit.'

'I'm good here. Right by the door.'

Warning bells began to peal in her head; his smile was too self-assured for her liking. *Dam-*

mit. Maybe he'd discovered a legal way to grant him victory.

'Just say it, Stefan.'

'Marry me.'

Holly stared at him as her brain scrambled to comprehend the words, tried to work out the trick, the punchline. Because there had to be one.

'Is this your idea of a joke? It's either that or you've gone loop-the-loop bananas.'

'No joke. I'm not entirely sure on the bananas front, but it makes sense.'

'On planet bananas, maybe.'

'Hear me out. If we marry each other we effectively cancel out the competitive element of the will because we *both* fulfil the marriage criteria.'

The thought arrested her and she moved further into the room, studied his face more closely. 'But we'd have to stay married for a year.'

'Correct.'

'What would happen at the end of the year?'

'We would co-own Il Boschetto di Sole. Yesterday neither of us thought we'd own even an acre, so why not settle for fifty-fifty?'

'Split it?'

'Yes. Why not? This way guarantees us half

each—I realise we'd need to figure out a fair way to actually divide the land, but I would be happy to do that up-front.'

Suspicion tugged at her as she searched for an ulterior motive. Was this some way to trick her out of everything? But instinct told her Stefan Petrelli didn't work like that.

Get real, Holly.

Had she learnt nothing? Her instinct when it came to men and their motives was hardly stellar.

'I don't get it. Why are you happy to do this?'

'A guaranteed fifty percent works for me. This way it also means I don't end up with a wife who will try to manipulate me. We would both be equally invested in the marriage and the subsequent divorce. This works. For *both* of us. If we have to marry, it makes sense to marry each other.'

Logic dictated that he was correct. Her brain computed the facts. She knew that her father would be more than content with ownership of any percentage of Il Boschetto di Sole. Plus she had to marry *someone*—way better to marry someone who wouldn't have power over her. But as she looked at him her tummy clenched at the mere thought of marrying him. She would be signing up to a year under the same roof as a man her hormones had targeted as the equivalent of the Holy Grail.

Grow up and suck it up.

This made sense—guaranteed her father ownership of the land he loved.

'This could work.' Deep breath. 'But we'd need to work out the rules. The practicalities.' Another deep breath. 'This would be a marriage of convenience.'

To her annoyance, she could hear the hint of a question in her tone.

Clearly so could he.

His eyebrow rose. 'Unless you have something else in mind?'

'No!' Though a small voice piped up asking *Why not?* This man was sex on legs, and they were attracted to each other. They would be sharing a roof for a year—didn't it make sense to take advantage?

Yet every instinct warned her that it was a bad idea. Stefan had freely admitted his only commitment was to a relationship carousel and she had no wish to climb aboard. What would happen when his need for variety came into play? If...*when*...she wasn't woman enough? She could almost taste the humiliation.

'This would be a strictly business arrangement.'

'Agreed. I make it a general rule not to mix business and pleasure. So, subject to working out the details, do we have a deal?'

'We have a deal.'

Without thought Holly held out her hand, and with only a fractional hesitation he stepped forward and took it.

Mistake. As she stared down at their clasped hands sensation shot through her and her body rewound to their kiss, imagined the heat of his hand on her back.

Quickly she tugged her hand free. 'I'm headed to bed. I'll see you in the morning and we can iron out the details.' With that, she grabbed her suitcase and forced herself to walk rather than sprint for her bedroom.

Stefan stared at the closed door for a long moment. Was this marriage idea lunacy or genius? Best to go with the latter. This gained him land in Lycander and a place to scatter his mother's ashes. It also gave him control of the situation.

The only issue was the thorny one of attraction—one that needed to be uprooted.

Holly did not fulfil his relationship criteria. She wanted a family, a relationship that held more than just the physical, and he couldn't offer that. If he couldn't pay he shouldn't play—and he shouldn't even have considered the idea that their marriage might be anything other than strictly business. He'd still been under the spell of that kiss. From now on in he'd make sure to keep his distance, and he was pretty damn sure Holly would do the same.

His phone buzzed and surprise shot through him as he saw the caller's identity. Take the call or decline the call? In the end curiosity won out.

He sank into the armchair and put the phone to his ear. 'Hi, Marcus. What can I do for you?'

Marcus Alriksson was Chief Advisor and one of the most influential men in Lycander—a man who was close to Prince Frederick, and a man who worked behind the scenes to help shape Lycander's future.

'Stefan. We need to talk. Any chance of setting up a video call?'

Hell, why not? It would be a relief to have his thoughts distracted from Holly.

'Sure.'

Minutes later Stefan faced Marcus, keeping his body deliberately relaxed as he studied the dark-haired man on the screen. The Chief Advisor gave nothing away, but his dark blue eyes studied Stefan with equal interest.

'So, Marcus, what can I do for you?'

'I want to discuss the situation with Il Boschetto di Sole. Will you be pursuing your claim?'

'Yes.'

'Good.'

Stefan raised his eyebrows. 'I'm flattered, Marcus. I didn't know you cared.'

'I *do* care. More to the point, Frederick cares. You and he could be friends. You choose not to be.'

That was not an avenue he wanted to go down. He didn't want to be friends with his half-brother—didn't want to be anything. He wanted to maintain a simple indifference.

Liar.

Deep down he still craved an older brother who'd fight his corner. Once Frederick had done that. Then he'd withdrawn. Stefan knew why—because Frederick had blamed his younger brother for Eloise's departure. Worst of all, Frederick had been right to condemn him.

All too aware of the other man's scrutiny, he dispelled the memories. Now was not the time.

'Is that what this is about? A call to friendship?'

'I want to discuss a deal.'

'What sort of deal?'

'I'll get to that, but first some background. Have you heard of an organisation called DFL?'

Stefan frowned in thought. 'It stands for Democracy for Lycander, right?'

'Correct. It is growing in prominence and support.' Marcus's expression matched his grim tone, and his dark eyebrows slashed in a frown. 'But I *will* take it down.'

Stefan emitted a snort. 'People are entitled to their opinions. *Everyone* can't agree with the idea of a monarchy. Months ago you told me Frederick wanted to allow freedom of opinion, planned to be less tyrannical than our father. Yet you want to "take it down"?'

'People *are* entitled to their opinions. But I have a personal dislike for those people who choose to express said opinions through violence and racism.'

Marcus pressed a button on his screen and turned it round for Stefan to see.

Stefan perused the site, quickly assimilating sufficient information to realise that Democracy for Lycander was an organisation of the type that turned his stomach: a group that incited racism and violence under the guise of freedom and democracy.

'OK. I take your point and I hope you nail them. But I'm not sure what this has to do with *me*.'

'Times have been hard recently. Frederick is doing his best to reverse the injustices perpetrated by your father but he needs time. Under Alphonse, housing, hospitals, education—every system—was allowed to fall into disrepair and the people are restless. The storm last year caused further damage to property, land and livelihoods. Frederick is still not trusted by everyone—is still judged as the Playboy Prince, despite the fact he is now married with a son.'

Stefan shrugged, tried to block off the unwanted pang of emotion. He'd meant what he said to Holly over dinner—this was not his problem. He owed Frederick nothing…owed Lycander even less.

'I'm still not sure where I come in.'

'If you plan to pursue your claim to Il Boschetto di Sole then I assume you're getting married?'

No surprise that Marcus Alriksson knew the terms of the Bianchi will—perhaps the only shocker was how long it had taken him to make contact.

'Yup.'

'Good. Then I have a deal to offer you.'

Not interested. Stefan bit the words back. Marcus wasn't a fool. He wouldn't have come to the table unless he was sure he had something concrete to offer.

'I'm listening.'

'Your marriage could be an opportunity for you and Frederick to mend fences.'

Stefan snorted. 'Don't play me for a fool. You don't give a damn about a touching Petrelli reunion—this is *politics.*'

'Partly. As I explained, Frederick could do with some support and the people could do with some positivity. You could provide both. The return of the exiled Prince... If you come back to support your brother it would show solidarity, and your acceptance and approval would boost Frederick's popularity. Especially if you gild that return with a wedding.'

'I'm not even sure I *do* accept and approve of Frederick and his policies.'

'Then come and see for yourself. Frederick and Sunita are in India at the moment. Come to Lycander—have a look. Then make a judgement call.'

'And if I approve? What do I get from this deal?'

'I want to use your marriage to bring you back into the family. Whether we like it or not there will be media coverage of your marriage, and there will be a lot of speculation about the will.' Marcus's face suddenly relaxed into a smile that seemed to transform it. 'My wife April...' Now his voice glowed with pride. 'She is a reporter and she assures me this is celebrity news gold. It will be played out as brother versus brother. Your story will be latched on to and revisited and I'm guessing you won't like that.'

'No, I won't. But I don't think there's a damn thing you can do about it.'

'I can provide you with a suitable bride and I can help orchestrate the publicity around your wedding.'

'I can do that myself. Hell, I could have a private ceremony on a secluded island and hide out there for a year. I get that you want to big up the marriage—make it a public spectacle for Lycander—and that you want the whole reunion and brotherly support. What do I get in return?'

'In return Frederick will restore your lands and titles, *and...*' He paused as if for an imaginary drum roll '...we'll give your mother recognition. Set the record straight once and for all—set up a foundation in her name. Whatever you want.'

Stefan's heart pounded in his ribcage.

Don't show emotion. Maintain a poker face.

But there was little point in faking either. He knew that many people believed the worst of his mother—thought her departure from Lycander had been an abandonment of her son and saw her through the tainted veil of rigged history—and he loathed it. This was a chance to vindicate her memory and he'd take it.

'Deal. But only if Frederick is on the level.' If his brother was simply a 'mini-me' of Alphonse, there was no way Stefan would play nice. 'I'll need to judge that.'

'Understood. The bride I have in mind is Lady Mary Fairweather. The licence is sorted and the helicopter is ready to go. You can be in Lycander in two hours.'

Stefan rose. 'Not so fast. I've already got a fiancée. I'm marrying Holly Romano.'

It gave him some satisfaction to see the surprise on Marcus's face.

Before he could react, Stefan finished, 'We'll talk again tomorrow.'

CHAPTER SIX

STEFAN RUBBED A hand over his face and tried to tell himself that two hours' sleep was sufficient. He pushed open the door to the living area of the hotel suite and came to a halt on the threshold. Holly stood by the window, her blonde hair tousled and shower damp, clad simply in jeans and a thick cable knit navy jumper, bare feet peeping out.

Desire tugged in his gut even as he recognised the supreme irony of the situation. This was his fiancée and she was completely off-limits. There could be no repeat of that kiss, no more allowing their attraction to haze and shimmer the air between them. For a start Holly did not share his relationship values, and secondly they now had a deal—one in which the stakes were now even higher.

For him it wasn't only Il Boschetto di Sole to be won. He could have all that Alphonse had taken from him in a deal that did not leave him beholden. And, even more importantly, he could win public recognition for his mother; set the rumours and falsehoods to rest once and for all.

But to do that he and Holly would have to play their marriage out in the public eye—something he needed to know she was on board with. It also meant they could not risk any complications, and giving in to their attraction would rate way up there on the 'complicated' scoreboard.

'Good morning.'

She turned from the window, her eyes full of caution. 'Good morning.' She gestured outside. 'Look at all those people out there…going about their normal business whilst *my* world has been upended.'

He moved closer, tried to block out the tantalising scent of freshly washed hair, the tang of citrus and an underlying scent that urged him to pull her into his arms and to hell with the consequences. But life didn't work like that. Actions had consequences, and once you'd acted you couldn't take that act back. Lord knew, *he* knew that.

So instead he stood beside her, careful not to

touch, and looked outside at the scurrying figures. 'You'll find that a lot of those people will
be experiencing their own upheavals and worries. But I agree—yesterday was a humdinger
of a life-changer. But it is only temporary. One
year and then you can have your life back. And
half of Il Boschetto di Sole.'

One year. Three hundred and sixty-five days.
Fifty-two weeks. God knew how many hours.

'And life doesn't have to change *that* much,' she
added hopefully. 'I've thought about it. I know
we have to live under the same roof, but if we
can find a big enough roof we don't have to actually *see* each other much. We could even get
somewhere with separate kitchens, or work out
a rota or...'

'I get it—and I appreciate the amount of thought
you've put into it.' Obscurely, a frisson of hurt
touched him, even though he knew he should ap-
plaud her plan. It wasn't as if he wanted to act out
happy coupledom. 'That sounds good, but before
we settle down to wedded bliss there's the actual
wedding to think about.'

'Yes. But that's not so complicated, is it? We'll

give twenty-eight days' notice and then we can
do a quick register office ceremony. Simple.'

'It's a little more complex than that.'

Go easy here. Clearly Holly's ideas for the wedding were a long way from the public spectacle
now on the cards.

Suspicion narrowed her eyes. 'Complex *how*?'

'How about we discuss this over breakfast?
And coffee?'

Coward.

'Fine.' Her forehead creased. 'Though I have
the distinct impression that you hope food and
drink will soften me up.'

'Busted.'

She sighed. 'Dinner does feel like a lifetime
ago, and I *am* hungry. But do you mind if we go
someplace else? Perhaps we could grab a take-
away coffee and walk for a while? I'd appreciate
a chance to clear my head.'

'Works for me.' A chance to move, to expend
some energy—perhaps the fresh air would blow
away the cobwebs of intrigue. 'Any preference
as to where?'

'I thought we could go to the Chelsea Physic
Garden,' she suggested. 'It's not far from here.

Every Sunday since I've got here I've explored somewhere in London. To begin with I did all the usual tourist places—you know, Big Ben and St Paul's Cathedral, which is awe-inspiring. I went to watch the Changing of the Guards too.'

Her smile was bright and contagious, and for an instant he could picture her, eyes wide, intent on watching the traditional ceremony.

She shook her head. 'Sorry—I must sound so gauche. It's my first time away from Lycander and I decided to...'

'Make the most of it?'

'Explore as much as I could. But I've also discovered lots of amazing quirky places, and the Physic Garden is one of them.'

So five minutes later they headed across the marble lobby, through the sleek glass revolving doors and out onto the cold but sunny autumn street. Russet leaves fluttered past in the breeze and the sun shone down from a cloudless sky.

They walked briskly. Holly made no attempt to make conversation and yet the silence felt comfortable rather than awkward. For him it was a much-needed buffer until they sat down to negotiate exactly how their marriage would work.

Fifteen minutes and a café stop brought them to the gardens, with bacon and avocado sandwiches and take-away coffees in hand. As they wended their way through he looked around, feeling a sense of tranquillity and awe at the number of different plants on show and their medicinal properties.

'We'll walk through the rock garden, if you like?' Holly offered. 'It's the oldest rock garden in the world, partly made with stones from the Tower of London and also Icelandic lava that was brought over here in 1772.'

Her face was animated as she spoke, and for an instant he wished that they could simply wander around and explore this place she clearly loved. That there was no agenda.

'Once we get through here, and then go round a bit, there is a secluded part where we can sit.'

Different scents wafted through the air, and soon they arrived at a pretty walled area and settled onto a bench.

Once seated, he unwrapped his sandwich and turned to face her. He waited until she'd taken her first appreciative bite and figured it was as good a time as any.

'So the wedding—there's been a change of plan. I've decided to go public with our engagement.'

She stilled, her sandwich halfway to her mouth.

'This is a good time for the exiled Prince to return to Lycander—I want to use our wedding as a publicity stunt to smooth that return.'

Lowering the sandwich, she opted for a gulp of coffee. 'When exactly did you decide that? You didn't mention any return over dinner. Or when you "proposed".' She tilted her head to one side, her blonde hair rippling in the breeze as she studied his expression, her blue eyes now wary, as if in search of a trap.

'I spoke with Marcus Alriksson last night. Lycander's—'

'Chief Advisor. I know who Marcus Alriksson is.'

'And we agreed that this is an optimum moment for my return.'

'Because Crown Prince Frederick could do with some family support,' Holly agreed, and suddenly there was that smile again. 'I *knew* you couldn't be as indifferent about Lycander as you made out yesterday.'

For a daft second Stefan wished he deserved the approval that radiated from her—but he didn't, and he wouldn't let her cast him in family-man mode, nor as a knight in shining armour.

'That is not my motivation. Marcus and I have made a deal. If he can convince me that Frederick is genuine about reform in Lycander then, yes, I will offer my support—in return for the lands my father took from me. No land, no support, no return.'

Careful here. He had no intention of sharing *all* the details of the deal he'd made, and he didn't want to bring up Eloise.

He forced himself to hold Holly's gaze, saw the flash of disappointment and steeled himself not to give a damn. He owed Frederick nothing. The whole point of severing family ties was the fact that they no longer existed—couldn't be used to push or pull.

'But my motivation is beside the point. The point is that it does change the parameters of our marriage. The wedding will now be a grand spectacle, acted out on the global stage, and our marriage will be under public scrutiny. In order to be able to offer Frederick support I need the

Lycandrian public to accept me—and you would
be a key player in that. I would want you to be
in charge of "branding" us as well, of course, as
being part of that brand. I will pay you a generous salary for that.'

That was the bunch of carrots. Now for the
stick…

'However, if this is too much for you take on
board, I understand. We can abandon our marriage plan and go back to the marriage race. But
I think it's fair to tell you that Marcus has a bride
lined up for me.'

There was silence as she thought, her hands
cupped tightly around her coffee cup. He realised
he was holding his breath, his whole body tense
as he awaited her decision. *Relax*. Worst-case
scenario: he'd marry Marcus's choice of bride.
Not his preferred option, but not the end of the
world either.

Turning, she looked at him. 'I accept your
offer—but I have an additional condition.'

'What?'

'If you don't have children I would like you to
leave your share of Il Boschetto di Sole to me
or my children. That way one day the land will

be reunited. It seems fair to me. You are asking for my help to win more land for yourself—this way my family will gain something in the future. Something important.' Her gaze didn't leave his. 'Of course you can refuse. Marry whoever Marcus has chosen. But I think you have a better chance of pulling off a "branding" exercise with me. Otherwise, I guarantee all the publicity will be about the "marriage race".'

Annoyance warred with admiration. It turned out Holly had a talent for negotiation too. Her request was unusual, but reasonable.

'Agreed.' No point prolonging negotiations. 'So we have a new deal?'

'Yes.'

This time she nodded her head, kept her hands firmly around her cup. 'But I'll be up-front. I *do* think you have a better chance with me, but this wedding won't be an easy sell. People will realise we are getting married through legal necessity. We certainly can't pretend it's a love match. Especially when we plan to start divorce proceedings in a year.'

'You'll need to find some positive spin.'

'Ha-ha! I'm not sure an army of washing machines could provide enough spin.'

Placing the coffee down, she tugged a serviette from her bag, a pen from her pocket and began to scribble.

'The terms of the will are bound to be published, so any story we come up with needs to acknowledge the legal necessity of our marriage. But we need to incorporate some sort of "feelgood" factor into it.'

For a few minutes she stared into space and he watched her, seeing the intense concentration on her face, the faint crease on her brow, hearing the click-click of the pen as she fiddled with it. Her blonde hair gleamed in the autumn sunlight, gold flecks seemed to shimmer in the light breeze. His gaze snagged on her lips and a sudden rush of memory hit him. The taste of her lips, the warmth of her response...

'Stefan! Earth to Stefan!'

'Sorry.'

Get with it, Petrelli.

'How about this? When I came to London a year ago I was intrigued by you—the exiled Prince of my country—so I called you up and asked to meet you. We hit it off and started a re-lationship. A low-key relationship, because that suited both of us. Perhaps Roberto Bianchi found out—we'll never know. Anyway, when we came to know the terms of the will we really did not want to fight—we even wondered if he'd been hoping we'd marry each other and that's what we decided to do. It could be that it won't work, and we both know that, but in that case we will each own half the grove.'

Stefan looked at her appreciatively. 'I like it. That has a definite ring of authenticity and, whilst we *are* fibbing, it isn't so great a fib as all that. Hell, it could even have happened like that.'

For a second his imagination ran with the idea. Their meeting, the tug of attraction… Only in this version it was an attraction that had no bar-riers, an attraction that could be fulfilled…

Whoa. Rein it in.

The silence twanged. Her cheeks flushed and then she let out a sigh. 'I think we need to role-play it.'

'Huh?' Given where his imagination had been heading, he couldn't hold back the note of shock.

'No!' Her flush deepened; pink climbed the

angles of her cheekbones. 'I don't mean every detail. *Obviously.* I mean we're going to be questioned closely on this. How did we meet? Where was it? What were we wearing? How did we feel? I assume part of this gig will involve press interviews and appearances on TV. So I think we need to have a practice run. I know it feels stupid, but I think it's important.'

Stefan shrugged. 'OK. Here and now?'

'Sure. Why not?' Holly looked around, checked there was no one to see them, no one close enough to overhear them. 'So... I've written to you, asking to meet with you. Why do you agree, given that you are known to have little interest in Lycander?'

'You sent a photo?'

'No!'

'Joking! I'm *joking.*'

'Well, I'm not laughing.'

But he wasn't fooled. There was smile in her eyes—he could see it. 'Inside you are. But, OK, fair enough. I can see why this is a good idea. But let's back up a step. What did you say in your letter?'

'Hmm... Let's work backwards—what would

have persuaded you to meet me? How about if I'd asked for help? For Lycander? Extolled Frederick's virtues?'

'I'd have told you to take a hike. Preferably a long way away.'

'All right. Let's say that's what you did and I took umbrage and demanded an apology. I turned up at your offices, sweet-talked my way past the front desk and...'

'You'd never have got past my PA.'

She glared at him. 'OK. I lingered behind a potted plant until she left to make a cup of coffee—or maybe she was on holiday, so it was a temp and...'

'You got into my office and I was so intrigued by your initiative I agreed to listen.'

'Perfect. We got talking and decided to continue the conversation over dinner.'

'Italian. I think we had spaghetti marinara and fettucine Alfredo.'

Dammit, he could almost taste the tangy tomato sauce, smell the oregano, picture her forking up the spaghetti with a twirl, her laugh when she ended up with a spot of sauce on the tip of her nose.

'And then a tiramisu to share, with coffee and a liqueur.'

There was a silence, and he was suddenly intensely aware of how close Holly was. Somehow during their conversation they had moved closer to each other, caught up in the replay. Now the animation had slipped from her face, left her wide-eyed, lips slightly parted. One hand rose to tuck a tendril of hair behind her ear.

She looked exactly as she would have looked on that mythical first date.

'And then this…' he said and, moving across he turned to face her, cupped her face in his hand and kissed her.

Imagination and reality fused. The surrounding scents of the garden combined with the idea that this was really a date. The kiss was sweet, and yet underlain with a passion that heated up as she gave a small moan against his mouth. In response he deepened the kiss, felt the pull of desire, the caress of her fingers on the nape of his neck.

He had no idea how long they kissed until the real world intruded in the shape of a terrier. The small dog bounded up to them and started barking, leaping up, desperate for the remains of Holly's abandoned bacon sandwich.

They pulled apart. His expression was no doubt as dazed as hers, and her lips were swollen, her hair dishevelled. The dog, uncaring, continued to target the bacon, and within minutes its owner had hurried up, hand in hand with a toddler.

The little girl beamed at them. 'Hello!'

Stefan pulled himself together. 'Hello. Is this your dog?'

'Yes. He's called Teddy.'

'What a lovely name.' Holly leaned down and patted the dog, which promptly rolled over and presented his tummy.

'He likes you.'

'I like him too.'

'Come on, Lily. Come on, Teddy.' The woman grinned at them. 'Sorry for the interruption!'

'No problem,' Holly managed.

Once the trio had receded into the depths of the gardens she put her head in her hands. 'I am *beyond* embarrassed.'

'The exiled Prince of Lycander and his fiancée—caught necking like a couple of teenagers.'

'On a bench over a bacon and avocado butty!'

Suddenly Holly began to giggle and, unable to help himself, Stefan chuckled. Within minutes they both couldn't stop laughing. As soon as his laughter nearly subsided he would catch her eye and he'd be off again. In truth, he couldn't remember the last time he'd laughed so freely.

Eventually they leant back, breathless, and Holly shook her head. 'I'm exhausted!'

Stefan glanced at his watch. 'And we've still got loads to do if we're going to catch a plane tomorrow morning.'

'Tomorrow morning?'

'Yup. We're headed to Lycander first thing.'

The words were a reminder of what this was all about. The reason for their role-play was to create an illusion, to enable him to keep his deal with Marcus.

'There's no point hanging about—especially as I want to pre-empt any publicity about the will.'

The private jet was already booked. Marcus had offered the use of a royal helicopter, but Stefan had been resolute in his refusal. Until he sussed out whether Frederick was on the level he would accept nothing from the monarchy.

'I can't just pack up and go at such short notice. I have a job and...'

'I am sure Lamberts will understand—especially given the publicity potential. If they kick up a fuss negotiate. Say you'll use them to help with the wedding.'

All trace of laughter had disappeared from her eyes now. 'Is *everything* a deal to you?'

He rose to his feet. 'Everything in life is a deal. You'd do well to remember that.'

CHAPTER SEVEN

THE FOLLOWING MORNING Holly unclicked her seat belt as the jet cleaved its way through the clouds. The whole idea that she was aboard a private jet seemed surreal; in fact the whole situation seemed to personify the idea of a waking dream.

The past day they had been caught up in a whirl of arrangements—conference calls with Marcus Alriksson, packing, planning, plotting… Oddly, the most real event had been their time in the Physic Garden. Great—how messed up was her head when that role play felt real?

A glance at Stefan and her breath caught in her throat. Damn the man for the way he affected her hormones. Their kiss was still seared on her brain—just the thought of it was enough to tingle her lips, send a shimmer of desire over her skin. But it was a dead-end desire and she knew it—it was imperative that she focus on reality. Actual cold, hard facts.

This marriage was to be undertaken for legal reasons and the wedding itself was to be a publicity stunt—a means for the exiled Prince to stage a return.

A sudden sense of empathy surfaced in her. If this was surreal to *her*...

Tucking a tendril of hair behind her ear, she looked away from the window and towards him. 'How are you feeling?'

'Fine.'

'Hang on...' Reaching out, she prodded his chest and a fizz jolted through her, demonstrating that their attraction was still alive and kickboxing.

'What are you doing?'

'A check to see if you're made of granite or some strange alien substance. Because, assuming you are flesh and blood, you *must* be feeling something other than "fine". You haven't been to Lycander in eight years...you're about to be reunited with your brother...you—'

'I'm *fine*. It's just a place like any other.'

But his gaze couldn't quite hold hers, and for a

tell-tale second his eyes scooted to the window, as if to gauge their direction, estimate the time that remained until they got there.

She shook her head. 'I don't believe you can be fine.'

'You can believe what you want.' He ran a hand over his face. 'Sorry. I didn't mean to snap, but how about we change the subject? Go through the plan of action?'

'Distraction therapy?'

'Whatever.' But his tone belied the word, held a hint of a smile. 'Let's just do it.'

'OK.' Holly ticked the points off on her fingers. 'First up, a meet-and-greet and a joint press interview with general questions.'

Stefan nodded. 'Marcus will be there, and his wife April. She'll take us off to coach us for the television interview.'

'What about Frederick?'

'He and Sunita are on a trip to India—they have an educational charitable foundation out there. I told Marcus I'd rather postpone the touching reunion scene until I've had a chance to look around...see if I want to support him.'

Holly glanced at him, caught the note of bitterness. 'You must be nervous about seeing him again?'

'Nope. He's just a person.'

'It doesn't work like that. Lycander isn't "just a place". It's the place where you were born, part of your royal heritage, and so it's part of you. Frederick is your *brother*. You grew up with him.'

Wistfulness touched her. If only *she* had had a brother her whole life would have been different. Her whole family's life would have been different. Perhaps her parents' marriage would have blossomed instead of withering; perhaps her mother would have loved her...bonded with her.

'That has to mean something.'

'Not necessarily anything good.'

His tone was flat, dismissive, and yet she sensed an underlying hurt. 'I don't buy the whole flesh-and-blood bond.'

'It's not about that. You spent time together— you shared a family life. That bonds you...gives you something to build on.'

Or it should. Sadness touched her that it hadn't worked that way for her—that her mother had been unable to find it in her to love her. Had been able to walk away and leave her behind without a backward glance in the quest for a life of her own.

Perhaps Stefan would agree that her mother had done the right thing? One life. One chance. Every man or woman for themselves. But at least he had specified that the mantra only worked as long as no one got hurt. Holly *had* been hurt, with a searing pain that had banded her chest daily in the immediate aftermath, with the realisation that she would never win her mother's love. Even now sometimes she would catch herself studying her reflection, wondering what it was about her that was so damn unlovable.

Stop, Holly. This wasn't about her.

'I just think that you should give Frederick a chance.'

'That is exactly what I *am* doing,' he said evenly. 'Marcus has arranged various visits and meetings with government officials. I'll be doing some of my own spot-visits as well. If Frederick is on the level I will uphold my end of the deal.'

In theory he was right. But she could sense his resistance to the idea that this could be more than a deal—sensed too that it was time to leave the subject.

'Right. I'm going to go and change.'

'You look fine to me.'

Holly glanced down at her outfit. 'I'm in jeans and a T-shirt,' she pointed out. 'I don't want Lycander's first impression of me as their exiled Prince's fiancée to be that I couldn't be bothered to dress up a bit.' She eyed him. 'And neither do you.'

It was his turn to look down. 'What's wrong with it? I'm still channelling the lumberjack look.' His smile was still drop-dead gorgeous, but his chin jutted with stubbornness. 'I am not going to play the *part* of a prince. I *am* one— whether the people like it or not.'

'So you're going for the accept-me-as-you-see-me approach?'

'Yes. I asked you to sell my brand—this is it. Jeans, T-shirt and shirt.'

Holly studied his expression, knew there was some undercurrent there that she didn't understand. 'Actually you asked me to *create* our brand.'

'Tom-ay-to, tom-ah-to.' He waved a hand in dismissal.

Royal dismissal, no doubt, that brooked no argument. Well, *tough*.

'You are asking me to help you win the support of the Lycandrian people. You must know that feelings are mixed about you in Lycander?'

'The people who hate me will hate me whatever I do or say.'

Why was he being so stubborn about this? He wasn't an idiot. What was his problem with playing the part of a prince? After all he had *chosen* to make this return from exile.

'What you wear is your choice. I can't strip you down and dress you in—'

Oh, hell. Had she really just said that?

'You could try,' he offered, and his voice was like molten chocolate.

'I'll pass, thank you.' Her attempt to keep her voice ice-cold was marred by a slight tremble she couldn't mask. 'The point is...'

What *was* the point? Oh, yes...

Narrowing her eyes, she erased the vision of a naked Stefan and snapped her fingers in an *aha* movement. 'When you went for that estate agent interview all those years ago, what did you wear?'

'A suit.'

'Why?'

'Because I needed to show respect. I needed to project the right image because I was the seeker, the supplicant.'

'Well, like it or not, that's what you are now. Not with the people who will hate you regardless, but the people who are willing to give you a chance. Show them that you care what they think—give them a good first impression. Once they get to know you then you can go lumberjack whenever you want. This isn't about proving you're a prince—it's about showing them what sort of prince you *are.*'

His jaw clenched and she sensed her words had hit home, though she didn't know why.

Then he shook his head. 'Point taken. But I didn't pack a suit.'

'Lucky for you, I did. Or rather I got Marcus to sort one out. It's in the back.'

There was a pause and she braced herself, then he huffed out a sigh. 'You're *good.* I'll be back in five.'

'Me too.' No point in Stefan looking the part if she didn't too.

Holly grabbed her case and headed towards the bathroom. Half an hour later she surveyed herself with satisfaction. She loved the outfit she'd chosen for her debut appearance as the exiled Prince's fiancée. Not too over the top, she'd blended designer with High Street. A pretty floral dress, with a matching cardigan over the top.

Right. Time to rock and roll.

As she re-entered the seating area her feet ground to a halt. The man was gorgeous in his uniform of checked shirt and jeans, but *this...* this was something else. The grey of the suit echoed his eyes, seeming to enhance their intensity, and the snowy shirt was unbuttoned to reveal the strong column of his throat. All she could think about was the encased power of his body, the shape of his hands, the unruly black curl on the curve of his neck...

Oh, God.

She swallowed the whimper that threatened to emerge. 'I approve.' Wholeheartedly.

The pilot's voice came over the intercom, announcing their imminent landing, and she hauled in a breath. For a moment their gazes held and she saw the sudden skitter of vulnerability in his.

No matter what he said, his nerves must be making their presence felt. Soon enough he'd set foot on Lycandrian soil for the first time in nigh on a decade. What had happened between him and Alphonse? Why hadn't he returned for his father's funeral or his brother's wedding? How was he feeling?

No doubt if she asked he'd say 'fine'. So there was no point.

Instead she stepped forward, placed her hands on the wall of his chest, feeling the pounding of his heart through the silky shirt material. She stood on tiptoe and gently brushed her lips against his. Stepped back and smiled.

He tipped her face up gently, the touch of his fingers against her chin soft and sensuous, and then he lowered his lips to hers, gently brushed them with his own. The sensation was so sweet, so tender, that she closed her eyes.

The plane jolted onto the runway, lurching enough to bring her to her senses even as his arms steadied her, ensuring she had her balance before he released her.

Then he held out his hand. 'Let's do this.'

CHAPTER EIGHT

As THEY DESCENDED onto the tarmac the smell hit Stefan with an intensity he hadn't expected. Lemons and citrus blossoms mingled with the tang of fuel, floating towards him on a breeze that had a lightness found nowhere else in the world. Familiarity hit him, and his head whirled with a miasma of repressed memories.

For an instant he froze—couldn't move, couldn't breathe—his gut lurched and he set his defence barriers at maximum in an attempt to quell the tumble of emotions that swirled inside him.

Images of his younger self—the iniquities and bleakness of his formative years, the anger and the pain and the dull ache of grief. The determination that the moment he could escape his father's control he would turn his back on being a prince.

And now he was back. Perhaps this had been a mistake.

A pressure on his hand tugged him back to reality. Holly's warm clasp offered comfort and gave him the impetus to move forward. Hell— he'd be damned if he'd show weakness. The exiled Prince would return in style.

A glance down at Holly strengthened that resolve, caused the fake rictus on his lips to morph into a genuine smile. He was back for a reason— to regain his rights, and most of all to vindicate his mother, set the record straight. He'd walked away from Lycander with nothing—he sure as hell could walk back in now. Stand tall in his mother's memory.

Scanning the crowd, he spotted Marcus at the back of a line of press, a vibrant redhead by his side, and then questions flooded the air.

'Stefan, how does it feel to be back?'

'When are you meeting Frederick?'

'Holly, how did the two of you meet?'

'When is the wedding? What about the will?'

'Why have you come back?'

The barrage pumped his adrenaline as he worded his answers, strove for balance, aware that each answer needed to be closed against misinterpretation and twist.

'Overwhelming…in a good way… As soon as possible, but I'd like our first meeting to be in private…'

Holly's turn, and she didn't even flinch.

'I moved to London for a couple of years and curiosity overcame me—I wanted to know more about the exiled Prince, and once I got to know him better I wanted to bring him home.'

Holly again.

'I'm sure you've all heard rumours about Count Roberto's will and its connection with us—we will explain it, but in an official interview.'

Marcus stepped forward. 'Time to break it up now, guys. I promise you'll have a chance to ask more questions in the next few days. Contact my office for the official schedule, if you haven't already.'

'Hold on,' Stefan interrupted. 'I think there was one more question. Someone asked why I've come back, and I'd like to answer that. I've come back because Lycander is part of my heritage. It's the place where I was born and where I grew up—it is the place that helped make me who I am today.'

With that, and with Holly's hand still firmly

clasped in his, he followed Marcus and April towards a dark chauffeured car.

Once inside the spacious interior, Marcus leant forward. 'Did you mean that last answer?'

'Does it matter?'

'No. I was just curious.' The Chief Advisor sat back. Turning, he looked at his wife and smiled, his whole face transformed with warmth. 'April will take you to your hotel now.'

'Yup. Ostensibly I'm doing an interview for my old magazine,' April explained. 'But I'll also be coaching you, checking you can pull this off.'

Stefan glanced at Holly, relieved that she had gone through their story in such detail. 'Sounds like a plan.'

Within minutes the car pulled up and Marcus nodded. 'This is my stop. I'll see you both tomorrow, for the first round of official visits.'

Soon the car pulled up again, outside a charming hotel-front, and Stefan inwardly applauded Marcus's choice—expensive without being in-your-face luxurious, just the right backdrop for a younger brother who didn't wish to upstage Lycander's ruler. The hotel had an olde-worlde charm—it was a converted chateau, complete with ancient stone walls, a paved courtyard and iron balconies.

They all climbed out, and there loomed the might of the palace in the middle distance. More memories crowded in—flash images of times he would rather forget. The enforced physical regime, the pain as he forced his trembling muscles into yet another push-up, another hoist of weights. Knowing if he missed his target by even a single rep there would be no food. And, worse, that it would be even longer until he saw his mother again.

His father's voice.

'You'll thank me for this one day, Stefan. You'll be a tougher man than me, a better prince. Tough enough so you won't fall prey to the stupidity of love. It never lasts. It never lives up to what you expect it to be. And it makes you weak. Look at your mother. Her life is miserable because she won't give you up. I would have given her wealth, prestige, but she wouldn't take it. Look at you— you show your weakness by your refusal to give her up. Your love for each other gives me the power, gives me the control.'

His father's words seemed to float towards him

on the breeze, echoing in his ears, and he realised that April was staring at him. But before
the red-haired woman could say anything Holly
had launched into a series of questions about the
forthcoming interviews and photographs, about
whether April would be covering the wedding.

They were questions that politeness forced
April to respond to, giving him time to recover.
This had to stop; he would *not* let his father con-
trol him from the grave.

'OK. Follow me,' April said. 'Franco will bring
in your luggage. I've booked a room where we
can chat in private and set it up to look like your
television interview will.'

Minutes later they were ensconced in a meeting
room. April sat herself on a comfortable leather
chair and gestured for them to sit on a small sofa.

Stefan glanced at the seat—it didn't look as
if there was any choice but for them to sit up
close and personal. Trying for nonchalance, he
lowered himself onto the red velvet fabric and
waited whilst Holly manoeuvred herself next to
him. Under April's expectant gaze Holly shifted
closer to him, the warmth of her thigh pressed
against his, and he willed his body not to tense.

'Right,' April said briskly. 'I know the truth, but I'd like you both to act as though I don't. As if you are on camera.' Green eyes studied them critically. 'You need to look more relaxed at being so close.'

Easier said than done.

'Show you're comfortable together and that you get reassurance from each other. Like you did when you arrived.'

Stefan blinked as an alarm bell rang in his head; he *hadn't* been acting when he'd descended from that plane into Lycander's heat-laden breeze. *No biggie.* He'd have clutched anyone's hand for reassurance when he'd been so stupidly stricken by memories.

'Let's get started,' he suggested.

April ran them through their first meeting and nodded her approval at the end. 'Good. Now, the next complicated question you'll need to field is: what happens in a year? Is this wedding just a legal necessity?'

Holly leant forward. 'We wouldn't have got married now if it weren't for the will, because it's so early in our relationship.'

'But you went to London a year ago—many would say that is a long time.'

Stefan shook his head. 'Marriage is way too important to rush into until you're sure. My father had four wives and he married each of them within weeks of meeting them. I'd like to think I've learnt from his mistakes.'

'Fair enough.' April nodded. 'But that still hasn't answered the question. What happens in a year?'

Holly intervened. 'Neither of us can predict the future; all we can do is wait and see and assess our relationship then. But...'

'Obviously we want a happy ending,' Stefan finished for her.

'That works,' April said. 'But you need to look at each other when you say that. Look as if the happy ending you're picturing is riding off into the sunset together—not waving farewell in the divorce court.'

Holly exhaled a small sigh and Stefan felt a pang of guilt that he had asked her to do this—go on air and fake a relationship. Without thought he reached out and covered her hand with his.

'Good idea,' April said with approval.

He tried to look as though it was all part of the role-play, reminding himself that Holly stood to gain from this too. Guilt did not have to come into play.

'So, next big question,' April continued. 'Are you in love? Holly, you go first.'

The silence went on too long. 'We're…um… certainly headed that way…'

'No, no, *no*!' April said. 'That is not going to work. You try, Stefan. Are you in love?'

Stefan met the green eyes. 'Absolutely,' he stated, but even he could hear the false bonhomie.

The green eyes closed. 'OK. That is going to fool no one. To be blunt, it's pants, and you are going to have to practise. Given the circumstances, you *will* be asked that question or a variant.'

'Fine, we'll work on it.' Stefan shifted on the chair. 'Now, can we please move on to some easier questions?'

April met his gaze. 'I'm not sure there *are* many easy questions. For example, you will be asked why you left Lycander. About your relationship with your father.'

Stefan could feel moisture sheen his neck.

'Then I'll decline to answer. I'll confirm what everyone knows: we parted on bad terms.'

No way would he bare his soul or the memories of his childhood for the media to grab hold of. He didn't even like sharing memories with himself—had locked them away deep inside. And that was where they would stay.

'And your mother?'

'I'll tell the truth about her. That she was a good, loving woman who didn't deserve the type of divorce that was meted out to her. But I won't be drawn into a big discussion.'

Next to him he sensed Holly's withdrawal, a movement of discomfort as if she were about to say something.

April frowned, glanced across at both of them. 'Is there a problem with that?'

'Of course not.' Holly's voice sounded sure, but he could still sense her tension.

'Good.' April closed her notebook with a snap and smiled. 'You need to work on being more lovey-dovey and then I reckon you can pull it off. As a reporter, I don't usually condone lies, but I have learnt that sometimes there are shades of grey and I think what you are trying to do here is a good thing for Lycander. But it *is* risky. So please be careful. People will be watching you; they will be looking for evidence of a break-up or a fake-up. There will be a huge amount of interest in you both and you will be subject to intense and invasive scrutiny. People will do *anything* to get information, because information is valuable. So stay in character.' April rose. 'I'll be in touch for another practice session before the television interview.'

'We'll look forward to it.' He made no attempt to hide the irony but April took no umbrage, merely smiled at him.

'I'll let Marcus know how it went.'

Stefan nodded. 'I'll see you out.'

Holly watched as Stefan and April exited the meeting room and exhaled a long breath. She felt as if she'd run a marathon. Her whole body ached from the conflicting signals she'd sent it for the past two hours. Pretending to be attracted to a man she was desperately attracted to but didn't want to be at all attracted to—the conundrum was testing her hormones to the limit.

She looked up as he re-entered the room. 'I've

asked the kitchens to rustle us up a picnic supper and bring it to our room,' he said.

To her surprise her stomach gave a small gurgle, and it occurred to her that she was hungry. 'That sounds brilliant.' She looked at him. 'You are very good at providing meals.'

The idea was a novelty. Ever since her mother had left Holly had taken on the role of cook, desperately wanting to look after her father, and the correct meals had become even more important when her father's heart condition had been diagnosed.

'Food is way too important to miss,' Stefan said.

'No arguments here.'

They made their way up the stairs to their suite, and Holly halted on the threshold. The suite was an exquisite mixture of contemporary comfort and historic detail. The stone walls of the lounge boasted a medieval fireplace, ornate gilded mirrors and beautifully woven tapestries. Latticed windows showed a view of the mountains in the distance and the hustle and bustle of the city below. The furniture was the last word in simple luxury—warm wood, and a sofa and armchairs that beckoned you to sink into their comfort.

So she kicked off her heels and did exactly that, just as someone knocked on the door.

Stefan let a waiter in and the young man pushed in a trolley laden with sandwiches, mini-pastries, slices of quiche, miniature pies and bowls of salad in a kaleidoscope of greens and reds.

Once the repast was arranged the waiter withdrew. Stefan seated himself opposite her and they both served themselves.

'This place is utterly incredible,' Holly said. 'Just the sort of place I imagined princesses living in when I was a little girl.'

'Is that what you wanted to be when you grew up?'

'It was one of many scenarios. I also wanted to be an award-winning actress, a famous pop star, a ballerina, an astronaut and a prize-winning scientist. The key elements in all these scenarios was that I'd win prizes… Oh, and for some reason I also always imagined myself arriving to pick up my prize in a pink limo!'

Perhaps that had been her own personal assertion that she was a girl and everyone would just have to lump it.

'What about you? What did you imagine yourself being when you grew up? I mean, you were already a prince.'

Stefan's face tightened and a shadow crossed his eyes. She knew her words had twanged a memory, and not a good one. But then he shrugged,

'I was never a real prince; that's why I left my kingdom as soon as I could. But I'm back now, and if we're going to pull this off we have some more work to do.'

Her tummy plummeted as she wondered if he was going to suggest they practise being 'lovey-dovey.' Not a good plan—not here and now, with her body already seesawing after the forced proximity of their interview.

'I think we need to get to know more about each other,' she said. 'The kind of facts you learn over time. So how about we do twenty questions? I'll go first. Favourite colour: pink.'

One eyebrow rose and his lips quirked with a small hint of amusement. She had little doubt that he knew exactly why she was rushing into a fact-finding mission.

'Dark blue. Favourite film genre: Action.'

'I'll watch anything. Ditto with books.'

'Anything sci-fi.'

Forty minutes later he stretched. 'That was a good session—and now I'm ready to hit the sack. Unless, of course, you want to practise anything else?'

'Nope.' As far as she was concerned the whole lovey-dovey issue could wait. 'I'm ready for bed too.'

In one synchronised movement they both looked around.

In one synchronised syllable they both cursed. 'Damn.'

There was only one interconnecting door.

Stefan walked over to it and pushed it open to reveal one bedroom. *Well, duh.* Of *course* they only had one bedroom. They were meant to be in a relationship.

'Um… I'm happy to take the sofa and you can have the bedroom.' Even as she made the offer she knew it was foolish—knew what he'd say, knew he would be right.

On cue: 'Too risky. Given what April said, I'm sure the hotel staff will practically have a forensics team in here tomorrow. The last thing we need is a story on how we didn't share a bed.'

'So what are we going to do?' Her voice emerged as a panic-engendered squeak.

Stefan frowned. 'You're completely safe, Holly. I won't try anything on.'

That was the least of her worries—she was more concerned with what *she* might do. 'I know that.'

'So what's the problem?'

Yet for all his nonchalance a tiny bead of perspiration dotted his temple and she could see that his jaw was clenched. Maybe he was as spooked as she was.

'The problem is…' *I'm scared I'll jump you in my sleep.* 'I don't want us to get carried away by mistake.'

'We won't.' Now his voice was firm, all sign of strain gone. 'We both agreed this is a business arrangement, a marriage of convenience. That is the point of it—convenience. So adding any form of intimacy into the mix would be foolish, and I'm not a fool. We're both adults. Let's act like that. We are hardly going to succumb to pangs of lust like adolescents. The bed is huge—plenty of room for both of us to sleep in.'

Stefan seemed totally capable of letting his brain rule his pants and she should be pleased about that. His words all made perfect sense and yet hurt pinged inside her, each syllable a pinprick of irrational pain. If he were truly attracted to her wouldn't it be hard for him to be so logical, so rational and in control?

Graham's words still echoed in her brain: *'Not woman enough...' 'Inexperienced...'* Maybe she wasn't woman enough for Stefan either—maybe he thought she was behaving like an adolescent. Maybe she'd got those kisses all wrong. Maybe what had been dynamite for her had been a damp squib for him.

'You're right.' No, no, *no*! That sounded colourless and flat, as if she didn't really believe he was right. 'It would be stupid to muddy the water when the whole point of this is to make it clean and fair. Entering into a physical relationship with each other would be messy—and I'm not a big believer in your type of sex anyway.'

'*My* type of sex? What the hell is that supposed to mean?'

His anger flashed now, but Holly didn't care. If he could sit there so calm and unbothered by the idea of spending a whole night next to each other then she might as well throw diplomacy out of the window.

'The kind that has no emotional context. It's negotiated physical sex. That's too clinical for me.' A part of Holly reeled at the sheer idiocy of this statement. But the principle was sound.

'I've had no complaints.' There was an edge of frost in his voice now.

'That's because you go for the sort of woman who is on the same page as you. I'm not.'

That at least was true. Stefan Petrelli liked variety—swapped his women out at regular intervals. That was not for her.

'In which case sharing a bed with me shouldn't pose a problem.' The frost had dropped a few degrees to ice now. 'I'm turning in. Would you like to use the bathroom first?'

'Yes, please.'

Perhaps a cold shower would help. She felt hot and bothered, mixed up, deflated, angry, relieved… Every emotion in the lexicon swirled inside her. Hell—they weren't even married yet.

Fifteen minutes later she was safely under the duvet on her side of the king-sized four-poster bed, flanked by a barricade of pillows, clad in flannel pyjamas buttoned to the top, eyes tightly shut as she simulated sleep.

The bathroom door opened and closed, then a few minutes later opened again. A scent of sandalwood, a burst of steam and she sensed him by the bed. Then there was a shift of the duvet, a depression of the bed.

Holly wriggled closer to the edge of the bed and waited for dawn.

CHAPTER NINE

HOLLY OPENED HER EYES, her synapses slowly firing into life. Warm. Safe. Comfortable. *Mmm...* Her cheek seemed to be pillowed on soft cotton underlain by a hard wall of muscle. Her leg was looped over—

Her synapses quickened and her brain began putting sums together...

Oh, hell!

So much for the barricade—somehow she had cleared that in a sleep-ridden assault and she was now plastered all over Stefan. Stefan, who— thank God—was dressed in boxers and a T-shirt. Probably because he didn't own any pyjamas... which meant he usually slept naked.

Suppressing the urge to leap up with a scream, she tried very, very slowly to disentangle herself.

Too late.

His arm tightened around her and then his body stilled. Clearly he went from asleep to awake far more quickly than she did, and his eyes opened to meet hers, his expression a mix of ruefulness and question.

Panic lent her speed and now she *did* move, rolling away in a scramble devoid of dignity and hampered by the row of stupid, *useless* pillows.

'Sorry. No idea how that happened. Sorry. I'm going to have a shower.'

A shower went some way to restoring her equilibrium—perhaps one day in about a hundred years she would even be able to laugh at the whole incident.

Poking her head round the bathroom door, she felt relief wash over her that Stefan was nowhere to be seen. *Chill.* It was imperative that she focused on the day and their trip to Il Boschetto di Sole. The thought brought a semblance of calm, a reminder that all this was worth it because it would enable her to give her father his dream.

She took a deep breath and went into the living area, just as the door opened and Stefan entered.

Goodbye, equilibrium. His hair was shower-damp, its curl more pronounced. He was dressed in a tracksuit and T-shirt and her gaze snagged on his forearms, their muscular definition, the smattering of hair.

'I went to the hotel gym—showered there.'

'Good plan.'

Silence resumed, and then he grinned. 'About earlier…'

'I'd rather not talk about it.' After all her protestations of being uninterested in his type of sex she'd made an utter idiot of herself.

'Don't worry about it. It's no biggie.'

'That's not how it felt to me.' Oh, God, had she *said* that? The innuendo was not what she had meant at all. The blush threatened to burn her up. 'I mean…'

Now his grin widened. 'It's OK. I know what you mean, but I'll take the compliment anyway.'

'Please could we just agree to forget the entire incident?'

But despite herself she could feel her lips twitch; somehow the sheer mortification had receded before the force of his smile.

'Deal.' There was a knock at the door and he moved towards it. 'I've ordered a room service breakfast—smoked salmon, scrambled eggs and pancakes—so we can talk in private. Hope that's OK?'

'Sounds good.'

Five minutes later she forked up a fluffy mouthful of egg and gave a small sound of appreciation.

'What do you want to talk about?'

'Well, we've talked about a whole lot of things, but we haven't talked about how we handle our actual presence on Il Boschetto di Sole.'

He studied her expression for a moment and she focused on maintaining neutrality.

'How does your father feel about it all? About our deal?'

'My father is honoured that the Romanos will own part of Il Boschetto di Sole.'

Holly remembered his face, and the awe that had touched it when she'd video-called him with the news. Once again a conflict of emotion swirled inside her—a happiness that she could give this to him, repay her father for the years of love, the years of bringing her up singlehandedly. And a selfish underlying of sadness that any hope of a career away from Il Boschetto di Sole had receded further into the realm of impossibility.

'I will need you now more than ever before,

Holly. Roberto Bianchi has given the Romanos a chance to create a dynasty of our own, entrusted us with the place he loved most. To pass on for generations to come.'

'Holly?'

Stefan's voice pulled her back to the present and she pushed away any thoughts of negativity. Until eighteen months ago she had been genuinely content to live her life on Il Boschetto di Sole, to live the fairy tale happy-ever-after with Graham, have children, fulfil her father's expectations. Once she returned to her home that same contentment would return.

And if it didn't she'd fake it—because she had no intention of letting her father down. Full stop.

Focus.

Stefan continued to look at her. 'Why do I get the feeling there's something you're not telling me? If I'm right you need to 'fess up. Because I do not want any surprises.'

Stefan was right. 'It's all a bit…complicated. My father is thrilled…*honoured* to be in line for part ownership. He believes the split is fair and that this marriage is an equitable solution. But I'm not sure how he feels about *you.*'

Her father had withdrawn behind an emotionless mask when she'd explained the marriage deal, that she and Stefan would come to visit him, that he would need to welcome Stefan as his son-in-law. He had agreed to play his part, but Holly had no idea how he felt about the idea of meeting Eloise's son.

'Why? Because he disapproves of me? Half of Lycander disapproves of me, so I can understand that.'

For a moment she was tempted to let him believe that, allow that to be her explanation as to why she was worried about this visit. But there was a bitter flavour to his words that she wanted to diffuse.

'It's more personal than that. It's because of Eloise.'

'My mother? Why?'

Now his voice was a growl, and she knew that this was a touchy subject. Hell, she could relate to that—her own mother was not a topic she wished to discuss. Come to that, she wasn't over-keen on talking about *his*.

'Our parents—my father and your mother— they were...involved.'

'Roberto mentioned that in my letter, but it was the first I'd heard of it.'

'Well, they were an item. My father loved her and she threw him over in favour of royalty.' Try as she might, she couldn't keep the anger from her voice. 'Broke his heart.' Thus doomed his marriage to her mother from the outset. 'In return for the crown jewels.'

Now anger zig-zagged in his grey eyes; his hands were clenched and she could see the effort it took him to unfurl his fingers. 'My mother was *not* a gold-digger.'

'Then why did she marry Alphonse?'

'According to Roberto Bianchi because Roberto persuaded her into it—he saw it as a grand alliance, believed she would make a great princess, and he wanted to scotch the romance between her and your father. Partly because of their social disparity, partly because your father was already engaged.'

'She didn't have to agree.'

'No, she didn't. But she didn't agree for the money or the prestige. She wasn't like that.'

His tone brooked no argument and his eyes were shaded with so much emotion that she stilled in her chair even as her own emotions were in tumult inside her.

Part of her wanted to howl, *How do you know that?* But she bit the words back. Stefan had the right to hold a rose-coloured vision of his mother, but Holly had no wish to share it. Her childhood had been blighted by Eloise; *she* had been the reason for acrimony, slammed doors and misery. So Holly had no wish to hear any defence of the woman who had doomed her parents' marriage. The only thing that might have salvaged it was a son. When that hadn't happened the bitterness had continued for eight years of Holly's life. Until Eloise had left Lycander; soon after that her mother had walked out.

'I know what you want to do, Thomas. You want to follow her. You never got over a woman who rejected you, treated you like the dirt beneath her designer shoes.'

Her mother's voice had been full of weary venom and Holly had put her hands over her ears in a familiar futile attempt to block it out.

'Go if you wish. But I will not be here when you come back, rejected again. I have had enough.

We could have been happy if you could have returned my love.'

'I always told you, Angela, that our marriage would not be one of love; it would be one of duty.'

'And it could have been happy if you had been able to let go of her, given us a chance.'

'I could say the same to you.'

That had been her father's weary voice.

'Would you have loved me if I'd given you a son?'

'Perhaps I would have cared for you more if you could have shown love to our daughter.'

'What does she have that I don't? Why do you love her when you can't love me?'

'She is my daughter—my flesh and blood. How can I not love her? Her gender isn't her fault.'

Holly had pulled the blanket over her head then—variations of that conversation had been played out so many times. But that time there had been a different end: the next day her mother had packed her bags and gone. All because of Eloise.

Holly tore off a minute piece of croissant, glanced down at it, rolled it between her fingers and told herself that none of that was Stefan's fault. Or his business.

'Perhaps we need to focus on the here and now. I believe my father has complicated feelings about this marriage because of who you are, but he understands the role he needs to play and he has explained the will to the staff and workers and told them the same story we're telling the world. All we need to do today is reassure everyone that nothing will change—that their jobs are safe.'

Stefan studied her for a moment, then nodded tersely. 'Understood. Let's get this show on the road.'

The journey to Il Boschetto di Sole was achieved in silence—a silence that contained a spikiness that neither of them broached or breached. The memories evoked by mention of Eloise swirled in Holly's mind in an unsettling whirlwind, and worry surfaced about her father's state of mind and whether all this would impact his physical health.

The car slowed as they approached their destination. Further memories floated into its interior as she rolled the tinted window down so the fragrance of lemon could waft in. The familiarity of the scent soothed her, calling up images of the beauty of the lemon grove, reminding her of times tagging along at her father's heels, racing through the fields of trees, watching in fascination as the lemons were harvested, loving the tart hit of the juice.

But there had been other, less salubrious times. Despair at her mother's treatment of her counterbalanced by gratitude for her father's kindness. The fairy tale of falling in love with Graham and the pain of the betrayal that had followed. Somehow now only the pain felt real, because the happy times with Graham had been nothing but an illusion.

A glance at Stefan and she saw his look of concentration, the way his eyes were scanning the surroundings as though in search of something. Perhaps it was an attempt to picture his mother, the girl she'd once been, the young woman who had apparently spent happy times here. *Eloise.* His mother. Her nemesis.

Sudden guilt ran over her—she hadn't even given him a chance to talk about Eloise. Eloise had left Lycander when Stefan had been a child—whatever her shortcomings, that must have hit him hard. Lord knew she could sympathise with that.

Almost without meaning to she moved a little closer to him. 'There are people here who will remember your mother,' she said softly. 'I'll make sure I introduce you. If you want.'

There was a pause. His grey eyes seemed to look into the distance, perhaps into the past, and then he nodded. 'Thank you. I'd like that. And Holly...?'

'Yes.'

Reaching out, he took her hand in his. 'About earlier. Whatever happened between your father and my mother all those years ago it sounds like your father ended up hurt, and I'm sorry for that. I truly believe my mother acted as she thought best, but I accept I can't know how it all went down.'

Neither could she. The realisation was ridiculously shocking. In truth, all she had was her own interpretation of her parents' viewpoints. Eloise could never put her side forward now.

The car arrived on the gravelled driveway and Holly saw that the entire staff had congregated to greet them. Embarrassment tinted her cheeks. 'Sorry… I wasn't expecting this.'

'No worries. It's good practice. In a few weeks we'll be on show for the world en route to the altar.'

'That makes me feel heaps better.'

'You'll be fine.' Stefan smiled, and all of a sudden, against all logic, she did feel better.

Franco opened the door and she climbed out, saw her father at the head of the group and ran forward.

'Papa.' Anxiety touched her—Thomas looked older than when she'd seen him a couple of months before. 'Are you taking your medicine?' She made sure she kept her voice low and the smile on her face.

'Of course. You must not worry. The past days have been very emotional, that is all. That the Romanos will own part of this… That you are marrying Prince Stefan… It is a lot to take in.'

'The marriage is for one year only, Papa. You do understand that?'

Worry began to seep in along with her sense of guilt. Thomas looked thinner, even his face was gaunter than a year before. She shouldn't have run to London. Since her mother had left she had looked after her father—made sure he ate, took the medication he needed to manage his heart condition. Provided he followed all advice the doctors were confident he could go on for many years. But had he been following the advice?

'Of course I do. Now, let us move on. Introduce me.'

Stefan moved forward, his hand held out, and the older man took it. 'Welcome, Your Highness,' he said, his voice full of dignity.

'Please call me Stefan. It is good to meet you, sir.'

'You too, Stefan.'

For a long moment grey eyes met blue, and Holly felt a jolt of something akin to her jealousy of years before. Was her father looking at Stefan and thinking of what might have been? That this was the son he might have had with Eloise? Was he wishing Holly away?

Stop. That way led madness.

'I thought you might like a tour.'

'Very much so.'

Thomas stepped back and smiled, though Holly could see the strain in his eyes. 'I think it would be fitting if Holly shows you round. Soon this land will belong to the two of you.'

'I told you, Papa. It will belong to *you*.'

'It will belong to our family.' He turned to Stefan. 'When you are done come and join me for a drink and I will answer any questions you may have. And of course feel free to ask anyone whatever you wish.'

With that he turned and headed towards the house. Holly submerged her anxiety, tried to quell the worries, suspecting that her father was overcome with emotion because the sight of Stefan had triggered memories of the past, of wandering round Il Boschetto di Sole with Eloise.

Later. She would speak with him later. Now it was all about Stefan and the creation of a good impression. Soon some of these employees would work for Stefan—men and women Holly had grown up with, people who had looked out for her and after her. Others she knew less well…a couple were new faces completely. But to a degree she held the responsibility for their wellbeing, and the idea was both scary and challenging.

She started the round of introductions, then

stood back to allow the staff to assess Stefan, watching with mixed emotions as their wariness and in some cases suspicions thawed as they spoke with him. Stefan was courteous without being fawning, and best of all he seemed genuine.

When he spoke to each individual he listened and focused his attention on that person, which allowed Holly to observe *him*. The way he tipped his head very slightly to the left as he concentrated, the glint of the autumn sun on his dark hair, the strong curve of his jaw, the intensity of his gaze, the firm line of his mouth, the contained power of his body.

'I have a lot to learn,' he said, once he had spoken with everyone. 'But I'll do my best to be a willing pupil. I want to get to know Il Boschetto di Sole, to understand how it works.'

Once the employees had dispersed Holly looked at him in query. 'Did you mean that?'

'If I am going to own it then I accept the responsibilities that go with it. Now, how about that tour?'

Five minutes later Stefan followed Holly through a mosaic paved courtyard and up a steep flight of drystone stairs cut into the mountainside. He came to a standstill as he gazed out at the panorama of terraced areas that positively burst with lemon trees, the fruit so bright, the fragrance so intense that he felt dizzy.

'This is…incredible.'

For a strange instant the whole moment transcended time and he could almost picture his mother here, walking amongst the trees, inhaling the scent, lost in dreams of a happy future.

Next to him Holly too had stilled, perhaps reliving memories of her own childhood. Then she grinned up at him, as if pleased that he shared her appreciation of the vista.

'It's pretty cool, yes? This is the last couple of months of harvest; some people say the lemons are at their best earlier, but I reckon these are damned good. Come and try one.'

She wended her way through the trees, surveyed each and every one, finally decided on the lemon she wanted, reached up and plucked it. His eyes didn't waver from her, absorbed in the lithe grace with which she moved, the way her floral skirt caught the breeze, her unconscious poise and elegance as she turned and handed him the fruit.

'Just peel it and taste!'

The fruit was surprisingly easy to peel, the burst of scent tart and refreshing, and as he divided it into segments and popped one into his mouth he raised his brows in surprise. 'I thought it would be more bitter.'

Holly shook her head. 'It's what makes our lemons stand apart; their taste is unique—tart with a layer of sweetness.'

He handed over a segment to her, felt a sudden jolt as his fingers, sticky with juice, touched hers. He watched as she raised it to her mouth and rubbed it over her lips.

'And the texture is pretty amazing too; they stay firm for longer. That's why—'

His gaze snagged on the luscious softness of her parted lips and suddenly all his senses were heightened. The taste of the lemon lingered on his taste buds with exquisite sharpness, the trees took on an even more intense hue; the noise of a circling bird was preternaturally loud. Holly had broken off, her blue eyes had widened, and he forced himself to snap out of it. Before he did something foolish…like kiss her.

'Why what?'

'It doesn't matter.'

'Yes, it does.' Shaking away the tendrils of desire, he realised it *did* matter. 'Come on. I'm really interested.'

She shrugged, continued to walk through the tree-lined area. 'That's why I believe we should focus on a different aspect of the business.'

'Such as?'

'Well, at the moment we stock the majority of Lycandrian supermarkets and we have a pretty successful export market. All of which is great. But—'

Again she broke off and he came to a halt. 'Go on.'

'I want to make it more…*personal*. I'd like to install a factory. Make products with the lemons ourselves. We could make lemonade, cakes… There are Romano recipes going back generations. My grandmother made the best lemon cake in Europe! And there are other dishes as well—really amazing ones. Lemon chutneys and jams… And I'd like to do tours, have a museum.

Honestly, the history of this place is amazing and the history of the lemons themselves is… It's really interesting. Did you know this lemon has taken hundreds of years to get like this? Originally it was a fraction of this size and inedible, bitter. Farmers were intrigued, though, and they crossed it with local oranges and eventually we ended up with this.'

'So why not do it? Take these ideas and run with them?' The enthusiasm in her voice lit her face.

Holly shook her head. 'The cost would be phenomenal; my father won't do it. I'm not sure he would want tourists here, or to be involved in making and selling products. To him all that matters is the production of the best lemons in Lycander.'

Stefan frowned. 'And he is to be commended for that. But in today's day and age you are right—other markets should be considered. You are the future of Il Boschetto di Sole and these ideas are good.'

'Maybe. But they need experience I don't have, even if I *could* persuade my father to implement them. You said it yourself—you didn't build your business overnight.'

'No, but I was starting from scratch. You already have a means of raising money. But I agree—you do need more experience first. So why not pursue the marketing idea? That would give you excellent additional experience on top of what you have already learnt. Why not ask Lamberts if they would train you?'

Holly shook her head. 'Because I don't think it would work. They've already offered me a trainee position for next year.'

'That's brilliant.' There was a silence and he frowned. 'Isn't it?'

'It's kind of them, but I refused.'

'Why?'

'For a start they're only offering it because of my new elevated status as soon-to-be princess. For a second thing there's no point. My future is on Il Boschetto di Sole. My half of it.'

'If you believe you can do the job it doesn't matter *why* they're offering it. Plus, this job would help with your future plans for Il Boschetto di Sole.'

'I really don't think my father will buy the idea.

Plus, I'd need more than a year's experience. Plus, I don't want to be based in London after our year.'

'OK. Then you could transfer to a PR company here. Even better.'

Holly sighed. 'Maybe I *will* do that one day. But not yet. My father wants me here…learning the ropes.'

There was something else. 'I'm missing something, aren't I?' he asked. 'I don't get why you can't do both. Have a job you love in marketing *and* learn the ropes. There's no rush. Why not have it all?'

'Because there are other things I want to do with my life as well.'

'Such as?

'Just let it go.' Holly's voice was low now, as they emerged from the shade of the grove.

'No.'

For a moment a warning bell pealed in his head. This was none of his business; there was no need for him to get involved in Holly's life choices. Yet he couldn't help it.

'I can see how much you want to pursue marketing, and use it to take Il Boschetto di Sole forward. I recognise that fire because I've felt it myself.' In his case it had been born of a determination to succeed, in whatever he undertook. For Holly it was a real passion, born of itself. *One life.* 'This is your life, Holly, take the risk. Go for it.'

'It's not that easy.'

The words ricocheted with an intensity that impacted him.

'It's no secret—you'll find out soon enough. My father is ill.'

'I am so sorry...'

Before he could say any more she waved a hand. 'It's OK. He has a long-term heart condition, managed with medication and a healthy lifestyle. But there is a chance he won't make old bones, and I want him to see his grandchildren. I want my children to have a shot at knowing their grandfather. Even more so now. I want my father to know the Romano dynasty will continue. I want him to see his grandchildren running around these lemon trees, watch the lemons grow.'

The words silenced him, because he could see her point, but... 'I understand that—I really do.

But your father may live for years. And to have children you need…'

'A father for them. I know.' Her mouth took on a rueful twist.

'Also, having children doesn't preclude having a career.'

'I know that too. But I want to spend time with my father and I want to be here for my children. Full time.' The words vibrated with sincerity, even with love for these as yet unborn children. 'That doesn't mean I don't agree with women working—I do. But for me it's important to give my all to being a mother. I can always go for a career later on.'

She resumed walking, and as they emerged from the shade of the grove he could see an ancient stone chapel in the near distance.

Relief touched Holly's face as she pointed to the building. 'Now would be as good a time as any to show you the chapel. Then we can decide if we want the ceremony to take place there.'

The topic of her future was clearly closed.

CHAPTER TEN

AS THEY APPROACHED the chapel Holly realised she had been so caught up in their conversation that she hadn't given a thought to the fact that this was her first visit to the chapel since her wedding fiasco. Not that she'd actually made it to the chapel then.

For a second her footsteps faltered. She wondered if perhaps she should have come here alone, to lay the ghosts of her nearly-wedding to rest. Yet somehow Stefan's presence made her feel better. His sheer solidity, his energy, reinforced the knowledge that it had been better to have the fairy tale shattered before the ceremony rather than after.

Graham had wanted to marry her for her family position, to have a job for life. Had never loved her. Their whole union would have been fake, built on foundations of quicksand.

As they approached the chapel an old familiar

sensation of peace crept over her. The ancient stone walls…the arched door with its honey-suckle surround… It was a place she had come to countless times when life's complexities had overwhelmed her—when she'd been small and hurt by her mother's indifference, an indifference that had bordered on dislike. Somehow the pews had given her comfort, and she'd studied the stained-glass windows, marvelling that those red and green and blue sainted figures had looked down and seen centuries, hundreds of people coming in hope of solace.

'This is a beautiful place,' Stefan said softly as they entered, and she knew from the reverence in his tone that he could sense the history in the very air they breathed.

As she watched him walk around she felt a strange warmth that he shared her appreciation of this hallowed place.

'It's always been special to me. My go-to place when life throws a curve ball.'

'I get that, and I would understand if you don't want our wedding to take place here. If you want to wait for the real thing.'

'I'm not sure if I'll ever experience "the real

thing". And somehow, because this marriage is for Il Boschetto di Sole, it feels right that we should do it here. This chapel must have seen countless marriages. Many of them will have been made for reasons of duty rather than love. Some of them will have been forced unions of misery and others will have been joyous.' As she'd thought *her* marriage would be. 'I think we should have the ceremony here. If you're good with that?'

'I'm fine with wherever we do it.'

'No doubt you'd prefer to have the ceremony in a boardroom, with an agenda and the deal written out carefully. *I, Stefan Petrelli, agree to marry you subject to the following terms and conditions.*'

Odd that she felt able to tease him, and his smile made her heart give a funny little dip.

Then his expression took on a serious hue. 'But really that is what marriage is—the ultimate deal between two people. You enter a pact to look after each other in sickness and in health. It's a deal. It's just a non-negotiable one that should last for life. Which is why I wouldn't enter it—I don't deal if I can't keep my side.'

'Does it bother you that we'll be standing here taking vows we know we won't keep?'

'No, because we both know that this is a one-year deal. It will be *With this ring I thee wed... for a year.*'

The phrase rolled off his tongue and she gave a sudden shiver. The enormity of those vows, even for a year, felt huge even as she reminded herself they weren't for real. They would be bound together for a year not by love but by legal necessity. Husband and wife. Any attempt to untie the knot before meant Il Boschetto di Sole would be forfeit.

'Is it bothering you?' he asked.

'A bit. I know we aren't lying to each other, but we are lying to all the people who will be watching.'

'Hah! Most of the guests won't give a rat's ar— bottom. And a large proportion of them will be laying bets on how long we'll last. Plus, how many people *really* believe the promises they make when they say their marriage vows? *Really* believe in the "ever after" bit of the happy-ever-after?'

'I'd like to think most of them do.'

'That is naïve. In today's age you would have to be an idiot not to consider the very big possibility that you'll end up divorced. Or that one of you will be unfaithful.'

Graham hadn't even waited to make his vow of fidelity before he'd broken it. 'Then why bother?'

'People figure it's a way of making some sort of commitment, but they know there's a get-out clause—they know they aren't really signing up for life. We've just agreed our get-out clause up-front. And I suppose some people get married because they want kids and see marriage as a natural precursor, the right thing to do.' He gestured around the chapel. 'For me, this wedding is the only one I will undertake. I know that. But you want the whole deal, and one day you might want to get married for real here.'

Holly shook her head. 'Right now it's hard to picture. I used to believe hook, line and sinker in the whole fairy tale. Now…not so much.'

'Because of the "complicated break-up"?'

'Yes.'

Holly hesitated. At some point they needed to discuss past relationships. Now seemed as good a time as any. No doubt the press would find out about Graham, and whilst she doubted it would feature in an interview, there might well be some coverage or commentary in the press.

'About that... It really was complicated. We were due to get married. Here, in fact. Then on my wedding day I found out he'd been cheating on me, so I cancelled the wedding.'

She looked down at the stone floor, traced a pattern with the toe of her foot. She didn't want to see pity or compassion in his eyes.

'That took guts,' he said at last. 'And in my opinion you did the right thing. If you tell me who he was I'll go and find him, bring him here and make him grovel.'

That surprised her enough that she looked up and met his gaze. She saw that his expression held nothing but a sympathy that didn't judge, mixed with an anger that she knew was directed at Graham.

'That's OK. I don't need him to grovel—it's over and done with. And, whilst I don't doubt your ability to make him grovel, you can't make him mean it.'

'I'd be happy to try.'

'It wouldn't be possible. In Graham's world he didn't do anything wrong.'

'How does he figure that?'

Holly hesitated. She'd never spoken to anyone about Graham's crass revelations. Yet here and now, with Stefan, she wanted to.

'The whole relationship was a con. Graham worked for my father and he saw a way to further his career. Marrying me would give him a direct line to the Romano wealth and prestige—a job on Il Boschetto di Sole for life, a house, prestige, social standing...yada-yada. He never loved me. I don't think he even liked me. But he pretended to and I fell for it. Hook, line and proverbial sinker. And the whole time he was sleeping with a "real" woman.'

'So what are you? An alien?'

All she could do was shrug and he shook his head.

'The man must be blind. Or stupid. Take my word for it. You *are* a real woman.' He leant forward, his expression intent and serious. 'You are beautiful and gorgeous and...hell, you are *all* woman.'

Shyness mingled with a desire to move forward and show him that he was a hundred percent right. To kiss him, hold him and…and then what? This was a business arrangement, and most importantly there was no future to this attraction except potential humiliation. This man liked variety.

But his words had warmed her, acted as a counter to Graham's betrayal, and for that she could say, 'Thank you. Really. I mean that.'

'No problem. I'm sorry you went through what he put you through.'

'On the plus side, I think I've learnt from it. It's shown me that love isn't the way forward for me.'

'Why? If you want love you shouldn't let one loser change your mind.'

'It's not that. Love made me blind.' And delusional.

She should have learned from her parents' example; love had warped their lives. Her father's love for Eloise had affected his whole life. As for her mother—she had loved her father with a love that had made her miserable, persevering for years in a doomed marriage in the hope that her husband would love her.

'It made me unable to see what sort of man

Graham really is. I think I'd be better off in a marriage without love. Finding a good, decent man—a man who will love Il Boschetto di Sole, who has a love and understanding for the land, who is willing to make his life here. A man who wants children, who will make a good dad.'

Because that was more important than anything.

She broke off and narrowed her eyes at his expression, his raised brow. 'What?' she demanded. 'Am I amusing you?'

'No, but I think you're talking rubbish. This paragon of a man sounds boring, and the whole idea of a union like that would be soulless.'

'Soulless? Just because *you* need variety and a different woman every month it doesn't mean a good, decent man has to be boring or a union with him soulless.'

'Where would the spark be?'

'There would have to be an element of attraction, but that isn't the most important consideration.'

An element of attraction? Jeez. A sudden memory of their kisses filled her brain—and she banished them.

'Physical attraction doesn't guarantee a happy, stable relationship.'

'No, but I'm pretty sure it helps with the "happy" part of it.'

'You can have an enjoyable physical relationship without love. That's what *you* advocate, isn't it?'

'Sure, but only on a short-term basis.'

'Probably best if you stick to your relationship criteria and I'll stick to mine.' *And never the twain shall meet.*

'Fair enough. But don't go looking for this paragon on *my* watch.'

'Meaning?'

'Meaning don't forget that whilst we are married we will be on show. If you find a suitable man don't follow up until our divorce goes through.'

There was a hint of steel in his voice and she narrowed her eyes.

'And does the same go for you? Because *that* is something we haven't discussed.'

'Meaning?' His question echoed hers.

'Well, what *is* your relationship plan for this year? We've agreed this is a marriage of convenience, but I'd prefer it if you didn't see other women, no matter how discreetly.'

His expression solidified to ice. 'I have no intention of seeing other women. I'm not a fool either. It would hardly do my image any good. And even if I were guaranteed anonymity I wouldn't expose you to that sort of public humiliation. I'm not as unprincipled as you seem to think. Liking variety does *not* make me a cheat. Whilst we are married I'll be taking my vows seriously.'

For some reason the words seemed to ring through her brain, taking the whole situation from the realm of the surreal to cold, hard reality. *Vows.* They would be standing up and taking vows. In this very chapel. Looked down upon by the figures in the stained-glass windows, watched by a congregation seated on these pews. How on earth had all this happened?

Pull yourself together.

'Good. I'm glad that's sorted. Shall we go and meet with my father now?'

Stefan entered the cool confines of the Romano villa and wondered whether his mother had been a regular visitor or whether she and Thomas

Romano had tried to fight their feelings for each other. There was so much Thomas could tell him, but he knew he couldn't ask.

Holly had made it clear that Eloise had hurt Thomas deeply, and he suspected the ramifications of that hurt had gone deeper than Holly had told him. In addition, Thomas was not a well man. So this visit needed to be polite but impersonal, kept to questions about Il Boschetto di Sole so that a fair split of the land could be devised.

He watched as Holly went forward to greet her father, saw the worry and the anxiety and the love in her blue eyes as she laid a hand on his arm, questioned him in a low voice.

Her father smiled, nodded and then moved forward to greet Stefan. 'Welcome to our home.'

'Thank you.'

He followed Thomas and Holly into a spacious kitchen. Though clean and sunlit it had an air of disuse, no smell of cooking lingered, and the surfaces were almost too pristine.

Holly glanced around and a small frown creased her forehead. 'Would you like a drink?' she offered. 'Tea?'

'That would be great.'

He noted that once she put the kettle on she went around and did a quiet check of all the cupboards. Her lips pressed together and her frown deepened.

Thomas Romano seemed oblivious to his daughter's actions, and instead focused on Stefan. 'So what do you think of Il Boschetto di Sole? I hope the staff were all helpful.'

'It is a truly beautiful place.' A place he knew his mother had loved…a place he would bring her ashes.

'Yes.' The older man sighed and then smiled. 'I understand from Holly that you wish to divide the estate between you?'

Holly approached the table, placed a tray with a teapot, delicate china cups and a plate of biscuits down. 'That is what Stefan wishes to discuss, Papa, but that need not be done today if you're tired.'

'I have already given the matter some thought.' Thomas turned his gaze to Stefan. 'I have looked at yields, at the economic and practical feasibility of where to draw the lines so that from a monetary viewpoint the split is as fair as can be. But there are other matters to consider. This place is a community, and I care about all the people who work here. Any split has to take their livelihoods into consideration.'

'Of course.' Stefan nodded. 'I understand that there are further considerations. I am sure there are places here that are meaningful to the Romanos.' He turned to Holly. 'I believe the chapel is important to you and I understand that—perhaps that should be included in your half? In return, I would like the Bianchi villa to be included in mine.'

The villa where his mother would have stayed.

Holly glanced at her father and Stefan pushed down a sensation of frustration. He did understand the idea of respect, but Holly was part of this too. Technically this was *her* decision to make.

'I have already included that in my proposal.' Thomas sipped his tea. 'I have also suggested giving you Forester's Glade. It's a place that your mother loved—Eloise said she found peace there, even when the decisions she had to make were hard.'

He grimaced suddenly and Holly leaned forward, her face twisted with worry.

'Papa?'

'I am fine, Holly.'

'No, you aren't. Have you been taking your medication?'

'Of course. I told you. I am *fine*.'

'I'll stay here tonight.'

'No.' Now Thomas's voice was authoritative. 'I do not want ill-founded rumours of my ill-health to circulate and I know how important it is that you and Stefan present as an engaged couple should.' He reached up and took Holly's hand. 'Truly. Holly, I am fine. But if it will make you feel better I will ask Jessica Alderney to come and stay.'

Holly twisted a tendril of hair around her finger. 'That *would* make me feel better. And I'll check in tomorrow.'

'Good. I will look forward to it. I have missed you; I am happy that soon you will be back here.' Thomas nodded to Stefan. 'Stefan, it was good to meet you. Please feel free to visit Il Boschetto di Sole any time. I look forward to your views on my proposal.'

'I am sure we can all come to an agreement.'

Rising, he held out a hand, shook the older man's hand and turned to Holly. 'You ready?'

'Yes.' Not that she sounded sure, and her blue eyes were worried as they rested on her father.

'Go!' Thomas smiled as he made shooing motions with his hands. 'I will talk to you tomorrow.'

Holly moved over to kiss his cheek and then followed Stefan from the room.

As they headed to the car she stopped, turned to him. 'Would you like to go to Forester's Glade?'

He halted, touched at the question.

'It may be a while before you can head out here again.'

'I'd like that.'

Or at least he thought he would. The idea sent a skitter of emotion through him.

As if she sensed it, she slipped her hand into his. The gesture felt somehow right and he left it there, clasped firmly as they wended their way through another terrace of lemon trees, the fragrance as intense as earlier. Once through this they started to climb a set of steep winding stairs cut into the mountain face.

A glance at her face and he could see that anxiety still lingered in the troubled crease of her forehead. 'I think you're worrying too much about your father.'

'That's easy for you to say. I know my father. Before I went to London I made sure he took his medication, ate right and followed the doctor's orders. Now he's on his own I am not at all convinced he is doing any of that.'

'He looked OK to me.'

Holly shook her head. 'Nowhere near as good as he looked last time I saw him. I checked his cupboards and they are all full.'

'That's good, isn't it?'

'No—because they are full of unopened bags of pasta, unopened *everything*. I don't think he's cooked anything since I left. I think he's been getting take-aways and he's done a big clean-up before I arrived.'

'Surely that is his choice to make?'

'So you suggest that I sit back and allow him to jeopardise his health?'

Stefan considered her words. 'Pretty much, yes. Sure, you can advise him to take care, remind him, but other than that it is up to him. He's a grown man; he is also a man with huge responsibilities on the work front. I can't believe he is incapable of sticking to a healthy diet.'

'It's not incapability. It's habit. He's just used to someone doing it for him.'

'Then hire a housekeeper.'

'He doesn't want to do that. Says he prefers family around him. Jessica Alderney is a friend— she's also a trained nurse and an excellent cook— but she isn't *family*.'

Stefan frowned. 'So you will live on Il Boschetto di Sole for life?'

Through duty. Do the right thing, marry her supposed paragon, have Romano heirs, look after her father. It was not his business—and who was to say she was wrong?

'You make it sound like a prison sentence. It isn't. *Look* at this place. Plus, my father is entitled to my support and my help. I love him and I have a vested interest in keeping him healthy.'

They came to the end of a small wooded copse and she stopped.

'OK. We're here. Forester's Glade—or Radura dei Guardaboschi.'

The view stopped his breath. The glade had

an aura of magic, conifers, a babbling brook, meadow flowers, a waterfall.

'I always used to imagine sylvan nymphs lived here,' Holly said softly. 'My father used to bring me up here sometimes when I was small and I'd play for hours. Anyway, would you prefer if I left you on your own?'

'No. It's fine.'

Stefan hauled in a breath, inhaled the scent of the conifers overlaid by the meadow flowers, looked at the verdant greens mingled with the deep copper brown of the soil, the blue of the late afternoon sky. He wondered if his mother had come here to make the fateful decision to marry his father—whether she had done it because she had been pressured into it by her guardian, persuaded to do her duty because it was the 'right' thing to do.

In so doing she'd made a grave mistake. And he didn't want Holly to do the same. Before he could change his mind, he turned to her.

'My mother…' he began. 'I know you have doubts about her, and in truth I don't know the history between her and your father. What I *do* know, from what Roberto Bianchi said, is that he pushed her into marriage with my father for the sake of duty. Perhaps she stood right here and made the decision. And perhaps she figured it wouldn't be so bad. Maybe she was swayed by the idea of the pomp and glamour of being a princess. Perhaps she did want to rule—to be the mother of royalty. Perhaps she believed she was doing the best for your father. Roberto Bianchi would never have permitted them to marry. Maybe she did what she thought was right. Just like you are trying to do.'

As he talked they continued to walk through the glade. They came to a stop at the edge of a cliff and he sat down on a grassy tussock, waited as she settled beside him.

'There is a lot I don't know—will never know now—but what I do know is that her marriage was worse than miserable. All the possessions in the world didn't change that.'

He didn't look at her—didn't want to see her expression of dismissal or disbelief. He knew that many in Lycander did still believe that his mother had been at fault. Instead he focused on the horizon, on the feel of the grass under his fingers.

'She didn't complain, but I sensed her unhappiness, saw how my father treated her—he made no attempt to hide it. Perhaps their marriage was doomed because she didn't love him. Because she loved your father. Alphonse claimed to love her, but it seemed to me that he treated her like a plaything—a remote-controlled toy that *he* needed to control. If she didn't comply, made a mistake, it made him angry. I saw the bruises on her. I just didn't understand where they came from.'

He sensed Holly's movement, her shift closer to him. Her body was close and so he continued, hoping against hope that she'd believe his words.

'So whatever her reasons for marrying him—doing her duty, doing what she felt to be right—it was a mistake. If she could have turned the clock back she wouldn't have made the same decision.'

'Maybe she would because she had you.'

The words cut him like a knife. 'No. I was the reason she was in my father's control—he had the power to take me away from her.'

He'd been the pawn that had ensured her compliance and in the end had brought her down. So it had all been for naught; she should have cut her losses long before.

'She loved you, Stefan. Be glad of that.'

Glad—how could he be glad when her loving him had cost her so much? *Enough.* This was not a conversation that he wanted or needed to have.

'Holly, just take heed. Live your life as you want to live it—you've got *one* shot. Don't waste it, or throw it away to do what is "right" for others.'

Holly sighed and he turned, saw the tears that sparkled on her eyelashes.

'What's wrong?'

'It's all so sad…'

A swipe of her eyes and then she shifted to face him, leant forward and kissed his cheek. The imprint of her lips was so sweet his heart ached.

'Thank you. For sharing.'

Warning bells clanged in his head. *Again.* A chaste kiss should not evoke an ache in his heart. Time to pull back—way, *way* back.

'You're welcome.'

A glance at his watch, a final look around the glade and he rose to his feet, stretched out a hand to pull her up. He noted the feel of her fingers around his, the jolt it sent through his whole body.

Make that time to pull way, way, *way* back.

This marriage was a business deal, and he had no intention of blowing it with an injudicious sharing of emotion.

CHAPTER ELEVEN

HOLLY OPENED HER EYES, relieved to see that this morning she was firmly on her side of the pillow barrier. A quick glance over showed that Stefan's side was empty, and she wondered if he'd even made it to bed. He had cited work the previous evening on their return from Il Boschetto di Sole, and remained glued to his laptop for the duration.

Part of her had welcomed the time to reflect, and part of her had wanted to hold him, to offer comfort after he'd given her that insight into his parents' marriage.

Guilt and mixed emotions had swirled inside her. She had grown up believing Eloise to be evil incarnate, the harbinger of all her parents' troubles. Now that picture no longer held good; the woman evoked by Stefan had been a victim just as much as anyone else. Another victim of love and duty. Could Stefan be right? That sometimes following the dutiful path wasn't the right way?

No! Her situation was a far cry from Eloise's. Her father loved her, and she wasn't in love with anyone else... The choice to look after her father was made from love, not duty, and she wanted a family. Yet doubt had unfurled a shoot, and she swung her legs out of bed, determined not to contemplate it or allow it to flourish.

Showered and dressed, she emerged into the living area, found him sitting again in front of the screen.

A continental breakfast was already spread on the table and he glanced up, gestured towards it. 'Help yourself.'

As she ate, he pushed the screen aside and came to join her. 'Have you looked at the itinerary for the day?'

'Of course.' She sensed the question was part rhetorical, part designed to indicate that today was all about business. 'We're visiting a nursery, a school and a community centre. Are you feeling OK?' Surely he must feel *some* trepidation about the day ahead; the idea of putting himself out there to many Lycandrians.

'Of course,' he returned. 'I'm looking forward to seeing if Frederick is making a difference.'

The statement had an edge to it, and she wasn't sure whether he hoped his brother was succeeding or failing.

The rest of breakfast was a silent affair, only today the silence didn't feel comfortable, and later, when they left the hotel, although he took her hand it felt false—she would swear she sensed reluctance in his fingers, knew it was done solely for the sake of their charade.

The car drove them through streets that spoke of the rich elite that Lycander was known for, filled with colonial mansions, freshly painted terracotta villas, but gradually, as they proceeded, the surroundings became dingier, evidence of poverty more and more apparent in graffiti and an air of dilapidation. Yet there were signs of change: construction under way, the hum of lorries transporting building materials, rows of newly built houses.

Still, the contrast between the glitz and glamour of Lycander's centre and its outskirts was stark indeed.

Franco pulled up in a narrow street outside a ramshackle building that, despite its lopsided air, did attempt a sense of cheer. The walls were

painted bright yellow, and a sign jauntily proclaimed 'Ladybirds Nursery'. Yet Stefan's face
looked grim as they emerged from the car,
stepped forward to meet Marcus.

'Does this building comply with *any* building
standards?'

'Yes.' Marcus's voice was even. 'I know it
doesn't look like much, but it is safe—and, as you
can see, the staff have made an effort to make it
look welcoming. The children are also looking
forward to showing you the garden at the back.
Feel free to inspect every centimetre of it yourself. It *is* safe or I would not allow it to be open.'

Stefan relaxed slightly, and his smile was in
place as the nursery leader came out with a group
of young children to meet them. A small pigtailed
girl approached Holly, curtsied, and handed her
a posy of flowers

Holly went down on her haunches to thank her.
'Thank you, sweetheart. What's your name?'

'Sasha.'

'Well, Sasha, these are beautiful, and we are
really looking forward to seeing your nursery.'

'I love it,' the little girl confided. 'My big sister is really jealous, because it wasn't here when

she was little. The teachers are really nice, and we have lots of fun. And it means my mum can go and work. "So everyone wins," she says.' She gave a hop of excitement. 'And we get lunch here and it's really nice. Me and my best friend Tommy are going to show you and the Prince around the kitchens. Is it fun being a princess?'

'Well, I'm not quite a princess yet. But I think one of my favourite things will be meeting people like you!'

Sasha looked up at Stefan, then back to Holly. 'Is it OK if I ask him something?' she whispered.

'Of course it is.'

Stefan, who must have overheard the whispered words, smiled down at her. 'Go right ahead— what do you want to know?'

'Are you like a prince from the fairy tales?'

Stefan smiled, but Holly caught sadness behind the smile.

'No, I don't think I am. But I want to be a good prince if I can. I want to help people.'

The words, though simple, were sincere, and Holly knew with gut-deep certainty that he meant them. That this wasn't all part of the charade.

'Now, Holly and I would love it if you'd show us round.'

Sasha slipped her hands into theirs and they entered the nursery. The converted house, though small, had been subdivided into four rooms, each one brightly painted, its walls covered with children's paintings and letters and numbers. Boxes stored toys that, though clearly second-hand, were serviceable and clean; the children were a mix of shy and confident, tall and small.

'We set up as a voluntary place after the major storm that hit last year,' the leader explained. 'It was somewhere parents could leave their children safely whilst they tried to cobble their lives together...rebuild their homes. But now the crown is funding this nursery and others—not completely, and we do still rely on donations, but we can afford to pay our staff something and the children get one good square meal a day. Now, I think these children desperately want to show you round.'

Even as Holly focused on the children, admired their work, laughed at their jokes and answered their questions as best she could, she was all the time oh, so aware of Stefan by her side—his stance, his relaxed air, the way he treated each child as an individual.

Once in the garden, the children proudly showed off the vegetable plots, as well as the sunflowers that stretched towards the sky with an optimism that seemed to reflect this nursery. Out of the corner of her eye she saw a little boy come forward, urged on by the pigtailed Sasha. But he pulled back and the two engaged in a spirited conversation.

Stefan had spotted it too and he headed towards them, looked down at the little boy, and Holly saw sudden compassion touch his eyes.

He leant down and spoke with them both. The words were too low for Holly to overhear, but she saw the little boy's face light up, then saw Sasha and the boy high-five.

Later, as they prepared to leave, Sasha bounded up and wrapped her arms around Stefan's legs. 'I think you're a very good prince. Better than a fairy tale one. And you *did* help.'

'What did you do?' Holly asked, once they were in the car en route to their next visit.

'It's no big deal.'

'It was to the little boy. I saw his face light up.'

'He and his brother were trapped in a building during the storm. A beam fell on his leg and now he can't play football any more. Both he and his brother are ardent football fans. Sasha wanted me to help cheer him up. All I did was say he and his brother could be the mascots at the next game of their favourite team.'

'That *is* a big deal. For those kids it's a huge deal.' Warmth touched her at what he had done.

'Yes, but maybe the house they were in wouldn't have collapsed if it had been built properly in the first place.'

'Which is why there is a whole new housing programme under way, and new standards and regulations are now being enforced.'

'My father has a lot to answer for.'

Anger darkened his face and she could sense him pull it under control, contain it.

'I think your brother is trying to do just that.'

He opened his mouth and then closed it again. She could almost see him make the decision to close the conversation down. To close her out.

He said politely, 'I'm sure you are right. Now, if you'll excuse me, I want to sort out this mascot issue.'

Two weeks later

Stefan glanced at Holly over breakfast, saw that she looked a little pale, with dark smudges under her eyes, and wondered if she too found it hard to sleep every night next to that damn barrier of pillows, knowing how close and yet so far she was from him. But, difficult though it had been, he'd stuck to his resolve—made sure he kept a physical and emotional distance from her when they weren't in the public eye.

Every day he held her hand, looped his arm round her waist, inhaled the strawberry scent of her shampoo, and every day his libido went into overdrive—only to be iced as soon as they entered their hotel room.

'Are you all right?' he asked. 'You look tired. I know this isn't what you signed up for, but you've been incredible.' She truly had, and guilt prodded him that he hadn't thanked her before. He had been so busy closing any connection down that he had failed to acknowledge her efforts.

'I *am* tired, but I've enjoyed every minute of it.'

He raised his eyebrow. 'Even the TV interview?'

'Fair point. *Not* the television interview. That terrified me and I'm still not sure we pulled it off.'

'We did OK.'

Hours of coaching from April had allowed them to put forward a pretty credible performance—perhaps the 'L' word had sounded a little forced, but Holly had laughed it off, blamed her falter on nerves and how hard it was to declare emotion in front of a global audience.

'Are you sure it's not all getting too much? Especially with the wedding plans as well?'

'It's not too much. Seeing all the problems Lycander faces, meeting the people affected by the floods, by the lack of public funding over the years, but also seeing how people cope in adverse conditions, how they pull together is…humbling. It's made me realise what a bubble I live in at Il Boschetto di Sole.' She hesitated. 'It has also made me realise what a great job Frederick is doing and how much there is left to do.'

'Yes.' Stefan refilled his coffee cup. 'He is.'

Like it or not, Holly was correct: his older brother *did* appear to be doing a sterling job and Stefan had no issue in supporting that. He had appeared with Frederick at some official events, and had indicated his willingness to continue to do so. But despite that the couple of attempts he and Frederick had made to spend 'brother time' together had been disastrous.

Not that he had any intent of discussing that with Holly. Not her problem, not her business. In truth, it didn't need to be a problem. Their deal had not included the establishment of a brotherly bond.

Aware of her scrutiny, he cleared his throat. 'Do you need any input on the wedding plans?'

Holly picked up the final flakes of her croissant with one finger as she considered the question. 'To be honest, Marcus and his department have done loads of the work. But there are a few things we need to figure out. For example, we need a song.'

'Huh?'

'The bride and groom start the dancing at the reception—take to the floor to whatever "their" tune is.'

'You pick.'

'Actually, I thought maybe we could put a different twist on it.' Holly hesitated. 'Did your mother have a favourite song?'

'She loved jazz—she had a whole collection.'

'Perfect. We'll have a jazz band. That will set

the right tone as well. And it will be wonderful in a marquee. Wait till you see the marquee—it is amazing. Just right to house the very impressive guest list Marcus has come up with, and the perfect backdrop for the wedding of a younger, returning royal.'

'Excellent. You truly are doing a great job.'

'So are you,' she said softly. 'You've won the people over—showed them that you want to bring about change just as Frederick does.'

A twinge of discomfort touched him. 'I do agree that change is needed, and as part of my deal with Frederick I will support his position, but remember this is all part of the deal. I am here to win my lands back, to regain my right to visit Lycander. No more than that.'

Holly frowned. 'I don't buy that,' she said. 'I saw you with that little boy at that nursery, and since then I've seen you interact with hundreds of people. You *do* care; you just don't want to admit it.'

'Don't kid yourself, Holly—and don't give me attributes I don't possess. I care about these people, but it isn't my responsibility to create change in Lycander or to undo my father's wrongs. That is down to Frederick. Once this year is out I will be returning to London and my life.'

How had this conversation got personal? Rising, he hooked his jacket from the back of the armchair. 'I've got a meeting with Marcus. Gotta run. I'll swing by and pick you up later for the luncheon with the charity commission.'

She nodded and he headed for the door.

Holly watched as the door closed behind him, leant back in the armchair and closed her eyes.

Get real, Holly.

Stefan Petrelli was a businessman. She must not try and imbue him with attributes he didn't have; he'd made it clear from the start that duty was an irrelevance to him.

A knock at the door pulled her from her reverie and she rose to open it, stepping back in surprise at the identity of her visitor. Sunita. Frederick's wife. Exotic, beautiful. Ex-supermodel. Fashion designer. Mother of the heir to the throne, three-year-old Amil.

'I am sorry to turn up unannounced; if it's inconvenient please say.'

'No. Come in.'

Pulling the door open, she stepped back and

Sunita swept in on a swirl of energy and vibrant colour. Her dark hair was pulled back in a sleek high ponytail and her vivid orange and red tunic top fell to mid-thigh over skinny jeans.

'I thought it would be good for us to meet un-officially. I also know how hard it is to arrange a royal wedding, so I've come to offer my help. Though I won't be offended if you refuse it.'

'No. Your advice would be great. Really use-ful.'

'OK. But before we begin can I ask you some-thing? I know about the deal—I understand that this wedding wins you half of Il Boschetto di Sole—but are you sure you're happy playing the part you're playing? Because if you aren't we'll cancel it.'

'Just like that?'

'Yes. Frederick and Stefan may be princes, but that doesn't mean they get it all their way.'

Holly couldn't help but laugh. 'No. I'm good with this. Really.'

'Good. There is something else I'd like to know. Has Stefan said anything to you about how it is going with Frederick?'

'You know that proverb about getting blood from a stone…?'

'Hmm… I also know the one about peas in a pod. Sounds as if they are more alike than they would care to admit. Frederick is being similarly reticent, but as far as I can tell their private meetings are a disaster. Enough that I think Frederick may bail on them soon.' Sunita wrinkled her nose. 'The problem is getting them to let go of the past—all those old resentments and feuds that Alphonse fed and nurtured and encouraged.'

Holly frowned. Perhaps she should stop Sunita there… But, damn it, she wanted to know more than Stefan had told her. All he'd said was that his mother's marriage had been miserable—he'd clammed up about what had happened after.

'It was awful for both of them when Alphonse divorced Eloise. You see, Eloise was kind to Frederick—tried to be a good stepmum—but as part of the custody agreement Alphonse refused to let her see Frederick at all. Frederick had already lost his own mother, and losing Eloise really got to him. Alphonse used that to pit Frederick against Stefan. And so it went on.'

Sunita sighed.

'Now they can't get past it. Even the Amil factor didn't work. I asked them to keep an eye on him and after an hour I went back, expecting them all to be in a group hug. But instead I walked in to find Amil happily playing in a corner and the two brothers sitting in awkward silence.'

'Surely they can discuss Lycander?'

'You would think so. But Frederick doesn't want Stefan to think he's blowing his own horn.' Sunita grimaced. 'Anyway, I'm out of ideas.'

Holly's mind raced, imagining a young Stefan and a young Frederick, both of them hurting and having that hurt exploited by their father. The man who should have supported and nurtured and cared for them had instead manipulated them, set them against each other. Stefan had been right. Alphonse *did* have a lot to answer for.

'I think I may have an idea…' she said slowly.

'I'm listening. And then I promise we'll move on to wedding talk.'

CHAPTER TWELVE

THE WEDDING TALK progressed over the next few weeks to the wedding day, which dawned bright and clear with just a nip of chill in the air as a reminder that autumn was well under way.

Holly gazed at her reflection, knowing that Sunita's expert help had provided the finishing touches to an ensemble that would hold up to any and all media scrutiny. Anticipation panged in her tummy as she wondered what Stefan's reaction would be as she walked towards him.

As a real bride would have done, she had opted to move to Il Boschetto di Sole for the past few days—to prepare, to ensure the groom didn't so much as glimpse the dress. Though she sensed that Stefan, unlike a real groom, had welcomed her removal.

The door opened and her father entered. A scrutiny of his face satisfied her that he looked well; Jessica Alderney was still in residence, keeping a strict eye on him, and he already looked the better for it.

'You look beautiful.'

'Thank you.'

'And, Holly, I wish to thank you for this; you are doing a good thing for the Romano family— past, present and future. Of that I am proud, and you have my gratitude.'

The words warmed her soul, made it all worthwhile.

'Time to go.'

He held out his arm and she took it, tried to quell the butterflies that danced in her tummy.

She followed him from her childhood home, then paused on the threshold and blinked, nerves forgotten. There, in full glory, instead of the horse and carriage she'd been expecting, sat a pink limousine. 'Papa…?'

Thomas shrugged. 'Did you not order this?'

'No.'

It dawned on her that the only person who could have done this was Stefan. She gave a small chuckle and suddenly the whole ordeal ahead felt easier.

The afternoon took on a surreal quality as she

climbed out of the limousine and smiled her well-practised smile at the selected photographers. Entering the chapel on her father's arm, she inhaled the scent of the fresh-cut flowers she'd chosen—a profusion of pink and white atop elegant stems.

The pews were filled with dignitaries and Il Boschetto di Sole staff. And out of the corner of her eye she spotted Sunita, bright and exotic in a golden *salwar kameez*, declaring her Indian heritage with pride, sitting next to Frederick, whose blond head glinted in the sunlight that shone through the stained glass. Amil looked adorable in a suit and bow tie.

Eyes forward and there Stefan stood—drop-dead, heart-stoppingly gorgeous—in a tuxedo that moulded his form, emphasised the intensity of his presence, his lithe, muscular power and the deep grey of his eyes. The black hair was nearly tamed, but the hint of unruliness added to his allure.

This man would soon be her husband, and she walked towards him now, watched by the world.

Remember Sunita's advice. Stand tall. Picture happy scenarios.

Il Boschetto di Sole in her father's hands. Stefan and Holly posing for the camera with a tiny dark-haired baby in Holly's arms. A girl. And they didn't give a damn...were engulfed in love for their daughter...

Whoa—hang on a second. What was *Stefan* doing in her happy picture? Idiot! Surely she wasn't stupid enough to delude herself that this was for real? Yet the vision was hard to shake...

At a gentle squeeze on her arm, Holly realised that she'd slowed down, that people were looking at her askance.

Come on, Holly. It had been a blip—nothing more. The important part of that happy scenario had been the baby. Stefan was merely an unwanted intruder, sneaked in by a brain that had been temporarily dazzled by this marriage fiction.

Reset button and resume walk.

She reached Stefan, kept the smile on her face, revelled in the appreciative look in his.

Fake, fake, fake.

This was a show for the public—a term of the deal he'd agreed with Marcus. The vows were a dream, the solemnity of the words underscoring her hypocrisy, and no amount of justification could quiet her conscience. All she could do was tell herself that she would make sure that some good came from this marriage—that it would benefit Lycander and give her father Il Boschetto di Sole.

'With this ring...'

Stefan slipped the ring over her finger, and as the simple gold band slid over her knuckle she felt panic war with disbelief. Fake or not, here and now, in this chapel, they had pledged their troth. And, even though she knew that the words did not bind them for ever, for the next twelve months they were joined as man and wife.

'You may kiss the bride.'

The words seemed to penetrate the dreamlike fog of the past half-hour and she raised trembling hands to lift her veil—though a part of her wanted to keep hidden. Stefan's hands helped her, pushed the veil back and then cupped her face. His clasp was firm and full of reassurance, his grey eyes full of appreciation and warmth.

Fake, fake, fake, her brain warned her.

But then his lips brushed hers and sweet sensations cascaded through her body until, in a mutual recall of their surroundings, they both stepped back. He took her hand in his and they made their way back down the aisle, through the arched stone door around which honeysuckle grew, permeating the air with its scent and outside into the graveyard.

History seeped into the air from the weathered gravestones and the stone walls and spire of the chapel itself—a place that had witnessed generations of happiness and heartache. Here she and Stefan, Prince and Princess of Lycander, greeted their well-wishers until they were whisked off for photos.

Her realisation that these photos would go down in Lycandrian history threatened to call on her panic, but somehow she kept the smile on her face, remembered all the coaching, placed her hand on his arm and looked up at him in a semblance of loving wife, absorbed in the way he looked at her.

Fake, fake, fake.

But her awareness of him was, oh, so real, and nigh on impossible to ignore with their enforced proximity. His nearness played havoc with her senses. Each and every one was on high alert,

revelling in the idea that for a year they were
husband and wife.

As the hours wore on, through the reception
and the four-course dinner, her head whirled.
Gleaming cutlery clinked, conversation flowed,
and the sound of laughter mingled with the pop of
champagne corks. Dish followed dish—exquisite
artichoke hearts, melt-in-the-mouth medallions
of wild boar, crispy potato *rosti* and simple but-
tered spinach. The marquee glowed, illuminated
by the warm white glow of fairy lights.

Once the food was cleared away, the jazz band
started to warm up and Holly looked at Stefan.

'Are you ready?' he asked.

'As I'll ever be.'

And so they went onto the dance floor, to the
smooth strains of a saxophone and the deep velvet
voice of the singer as he crooned out the words.
She'd hoped that dancing to jazz wouldn't be as
tactile as to any other music, but in fact it was
worse. The sensual sway of their movements, the
to and fro, the distance and the proximity, messed
further with her head.

Was he equally affected? Every instinct told
her that he was. Each time he pulled her into his

body she could sense the heat rising in him, see the scorch of desire in his eyes as they focused solely on her. When his hands spanned her waist, circling the wide belt of satin, she felt lighter than air—and yet heavy desire pooled in her gut.

Finally the first dance came to an end and they moved off the dance floor. She kept a smile pinned to her lips even as her head whirled. He walked beside her, coiled taut, and she knew his body was as tense as her own.

'How long until we leave for our honeymoon?' he asked, his voice a rasp.

She gave a shaky laugh. A laugh that tapered off as the word 'honeymoon' permeated her desire-hazed brain.

'About the honeymoon...'

'Yes. We agreed on Paris—nice and clichéd, plenty of romantic social media opportunities.'

Desire faded into a background hum as she met his gaze a touch apprehensively. 'There may have been a slight change of plan.'

Now an eyebrow was raised. 'Define "slight".'

'Actually, do you think we could discuss it later? People are watching us now and we need to mingle.'

Coward.

Perhaps, but it would be foolhardy to spark a potential argument now.

There was a pause and then he nodded. 'OK. I'll look forward to my surprise destination.'

Three hours and much mingling later, they were once more in the back of the pink limousine. Stefan handed Holly a glass of pink champagne—her first of the whole day. His too, for that matter.

'To pink limos,' she said. 'I haven't had a chance to say thank you. It's fabulous.'

'I'm glad you like it. I gather it is not, however, taking us to the airport so we can catch a plane to Paris?'

'No…' Holly took a deep breath and apprehension returned to her blue eyes.

As the silence stretched he took the time to study her. She had changed out of her wedding dress into her 'going away outfit'. A simple cream linen dress. Her hair now hung loose in all its golden glory, and she still looked every bit as beautiful as she had when she'd walked down the aisle, a vision in ivory satin and lace.

'You're going to have to tell me some time,' he pointed out.

She took another sip of champagne—presumably for fortification. 'We aren't going anywhere. We're staying here.'

Stefan closed his eyes and then opened them again, pinched the bridge of his nose and focused on keeping his voice calm. 'Why?'

'Because the past few weeks have all been about being in the public eye, being on show. I thought it might be nice to explore Lycander differently. I reckon it would look good to the public as well—fit well with the "returning prince" theme. What do you think?'

He thought she wasn't speaking the whole truth; there was something in the way her gaze had fluttered away from his for an instant.

'Wouldn't you like to go to Paris? Explore there.'

'One day I would, yes.'

Damn it. Maybe she didn't want to go there on a fake honeymoon; maybe she wanted to save Paris for when she could do the clichéd romance for real.

'But now you want to remain in Lycander?'

'Yes. I've realised that even though I have lived

here all my life there are still so many places I haven't seen—and I think it will be fun.'

A study of her expression yielded nothing but apparent sincerity, and he did believe her. He recalled how she had described her exploration of London. But he suspected there was an additional ulterior motive, and wariness banded his chest at the idea he was being manipulated in some way.

Well, if he was then he'd never give something for nothing. He shrugged. 'OK. If that's what you want. We can find Lycander's equivalent of the Chelsea Physic Garden. But I want something in return.'

It was her turn to look suspicious, and her forehead creased as she sipped her drink and looked at him narrow-eyed over the rim of the glass. 'Like what?'

'Take the marketing role at Lamberts.'

'Jeez. Why can't you let that go? We've been through it. There is no point—I will be taking up residence on Il Boschetto di Sole in a year.'

'I understand that; I am simply suggesting that this year you take the chance to do a job you enjoy—give it a try. It will be good experience that will help with Il Boschetto di Sole. One year. Where is the harm in that?'

Holly hesitated, twisting a tendril of hair around her finger. She considered his words and then suddenly she grinned. 'What the hell? You're right. Why not? I *can't* live on Il Boschetto di Sole during our marriage, and I *do* want to try marketing, and it *will* be good experience. I'll do it.'

'Good.' He raised his glass and a smile tilted his lips. 'To your new job.' And to his private hope that it would be the first step for Holly to veer from the path of tradition and duty. 'It's important to enjoy life—grab the good times whilst you can.'

This he knew.

And just like that the atmosphere in the limousine subtly changed. The air became charged with a shimmer of awareness—he'd swear he could almost see it—a pink glitter of desire. And he knew that really all their talk had simply been to put off an inevitable decision—a decision they had been headed for ever since he'd seen her walk down the aisle…ever since he'd lifted her veil and kissed her.

Holly stilled, her blue eyes wide as their gazes met and locked. Then slowly—so slowly, so tentatively—she shifted across the seat. The swish of her dress against the pink leather mesmerised him.

There was no need for words; instead he cupped her face in his hands and brushed his lips against hers, the movement so natural, so right, that he let out a small groan as her lips parted beneath his.

The kiss seemed timeless. It could have been seconds or it could have been hours before the limo glided to a halt. By then he was gripped with a desire so deep he ached, and he felt her answering need in the press of her body against his, the tangle of her fingers in his hair.

As they emerged, hand in hand, he tugged her towards the revolving door of the hotel, through the lobby and towards the stairs. Once inside their suite they didn't—couldn't—wait. His jacket fell to the floor and her fingers fumbled with the buttons of his shirt, crept underneath the material, and as she touched his chest, he exhaled a pent-up breath.

The words of their vows rang through his head:

'With my body I thee worship.' And without further ado he scooped her up and carried her to the bedroom.

Holly opened her eyes, turned to look for Stefan and saw the empty bed. Her languorous happiness started to fade and for a moment she clung to it, allowed herself the memory of the previous night. Laughter, joy, passion, gentleness... The swoop and soar of desire and fulfilment.

Her face flushed and she suddenly wondered exactly how to face him. But she had to—she had plans for the day...plans she was determined to see through.

Swinging her legs out of bed, she felt gratitude that he had discreetly exited, saving her an undignified scramble for clothes. Far better to face him clothed. Unless, of course, he had left because he was worried she'd request a replay. What if she hadn't measured up? Hadn't been woman enough? No—that was foolish. Last night had been magical—she knew it.

Yet that certainty dipped as she entered the living area. He looked so gorgeous and yet so remote that for a crazy moment she wondered if she'd imagined the previous night.

'Hey...'

'Hey.'

Misgivings continued to smite her. There was a grim set to his mouth, and his lips strained up into a smile that did not match the cool glint in his eyes.

'We need to talk.'

'Sure.'

His fingers drummed against his thigh and she could sense his frustration.

'Last night... I'm sorry... It shouldn't have happened like that.'

The onset of hurt began to pool inside her tummy, and she focused on keeping all emotion from her face and her voice. 'How *should* it have happened?'

'I should have checked that it was really what you wanted.'

'I think it was pretty clear what I wanted.'

'I meant in the longer term. We decided that we didn't want this relationship to become physical. Last night it did—without either of us considering the consequences.'

'We used protection.'

'That isn't what I meant. I meant the consequences to our marriage of convenience, to our deal.'

'So you regret last night?' Damn it, she hoped that hadn't been a tremor in her voice.

'No, I don't. But I do regret that we didn't figure out the rules first. Now we need to decide what happens from here.'

What *did* she want? Right now her body still strummed in the aftermath of the previous hours, and it was telling her in no uncertain terms that it really *didn't* want to give up that sort of pleasure.

'You said to me that you believe relationships with a time limit work—relationships based around physical fulfilment and a bit of sparkle over the dinner table occasionally. We could do that.'

'And *you* said that that sort of relationship wasn't for you. I think you may have mentioned "clinical sex".'

'Yes... Well, it turns out I may have been wrong about that. Turns out clinical sex is right up my street.'

Her words pulled the glimpse of a smile from him before the grimness returned.

'This isn't *about* that, though. The point is this is not the type of relationship you want and I knew that. So last night should not have happened. You are looking for a real husband, a father for your children, and I am *not* that person.'

'I know that—and I knew that last night. If I hadn't wanted to go ahead I would have said so. You are right that I want a real marriage and a family, a man who shares my values and beliefs. You don't—and I get that. But right now you are in my life and we *do* have some sort of attraction thing going on.'

She hauled in a breath.

'So last night happened and I don't regret it. As you said, the question is where do we go from here?'

Stefan has a point! yelled a voice in the back of her head. *This is not what you want—imagine the humiliation when he tires of you.*

I may tire of him.

Yeah, right. Dream on.

Fine.

'I think we should have a very short-term relationship—just for the honeymoon. Once we get back to London we'll live separate lives for the year.'

He hesitated, searched her face as if he wished he could penetrate her very soul. 'You are sure that is what you want?'

'Yes.' This was under *her* control—*she* was putting the time limit on it. This way she couldn't get hurt and she would get to replay last night. Win-win, right? 'But only if you do.'

'Oh, I *definitely* do.'

Finally his face relaxed into a grin that curled her toes and sent a thrill of anticipation through her entire body.

'In fact, why don't I show you *exactly* how much I want this? Want *you*.'

Temptation beckoned, but she shook her head. 'No can do. I have a plan for the day. We need to get going.'

'Get going to where?'

'Xanos Island.'

The smile dropped from his lips but she soldiered on. 'Sunita mentioned it. She said it's an amazing little island, completely secluded, with sand, rocks, caves—the works. I've figured out the tides, a boat awaits us, and we have the most amazing picnic ever.'

'Did Sunita say anything else about it?'

'Yes.' There was no point lying about it. 'She said Eloise used to take you there.'

'So you figured it was a good place to go to?'

'Yes.'

Because she thought the best way for him to let go of the past might be to revisit the good bits of it. He might not have had many good bits, but it seemed clear that he and Eloise had shared a few happy years before the divorce and its horrors. More than that, so had he and Frederick, under Eloise's guidance.

'I thought you might like to revisit some of your good childhood memories. I know there may not be many of them, but that makes them all the more precious.' She hauled in breath. 'And it's not only for you—it's for me as well.'

'How so?'

'I told you that your mother broke my father's heart when she married your father. But the repercussions went deeper than that. My mother loved my father and she couldn't deal with his relationship with Eloise. Couldn't deal with the fact that my father didn't really love *her*. So she hated your mother with real venom—and I was brought up to do the same. To me, your mother was the wicked witch incarnate and I never questioned that.'

It hadn't taken the young Holly long to figure out that the best way to win a crumb of her mother's attention, if not her affection, had been to insult Eloise.

'I'd like to make amends—go somewhere like Xanos Island and remember Eloise differently.'

Stefan met her gaze and then he nodded. 'Thank you. For feeling able to give her memory a chance. I truly don't believe she wanted to hurt anyone. And she wouldn't have wanted the fall-out to hurt *you*—I know first-hand how horrible it is to be a child caught in the web of your parents' destructive marriage. I'm sorry you went through that and so would she be.'

He rose.

'Xanos Island here we come.'

As the small red and white motorboat bobbed over the waves Stefan could picture his younger self, recall the sheer joy of being on a real boat, singing a sea shanty with the Captain and his mother joining in, the soft lilt of her voice helping him with the words.

But it hadn't only been the three of them singing—it had been Frederick as well. The memory, long buried, slipped into focus. His five-year-old self sitting on Frederick's lap, leaning over the side, safe in the knowledge that his older brother held him secure around the waist as he trailed his fingers in the water.

Enough. That had been then. Before the horror of the divorce. Before Eloise's departure. Before his father's *'toughen Stefan up and make him a prince'* notions. Before the anger and the blame in his brother's eyes. Before the emotions he couldn't forget, followed by his brother's utter lack of support through his father's *'make Stefan a prince'* regime.

Hell, he was trying, but each meeting with Frederick was so damned awkward—there was a vibe of anger, of strain, that neither of them seemed able to circumvent. Not that it mattered. As long as they continued to pull off a public pretence of civility that was all that was needed. All that he'd signed up to.

The Captain steered the boat to a small harbour and Stefan followed Holly onto the wooden jetty, hauling the picnic basket with him, and soon they were crossing golden sands.

'It's magic,' Holly said as they came to a halt. 'It feels like it's a million miles from anywhere.'

The sea seemed impossibly blue and the waves lapped gently against the sands. Flecks of sunlight dotted the green fronds of the palm trees that dotted the beach.

'I think that's why my mother loved it here: the seclusion gave her peace. I remember the last time we came here...'

The scene was vivid. The present faded and Eloise seemed to shimmer in front of him, kneeling in the sand, making a reluctant Frederick apply sun lotion, helping build a sandcastle.

'Frederick ran off to explore the caves and I had a monster tantrum because my mother wouldn't let me go with him—said it was too dangerous. I lost it, but she didn't—she didn't even raise her voice.'

She never had... It had almost been as if she'd known their time together was limited.

'Instead she hugged me, told me that when I

was older we'd explore the caves together. It never happened.' It was a promise she hadn't been able to keep. 'This is the first time I've been back since then.'

'Then let's go and explore now.'

'You sure?'

Holly raised her eyebrows. 'I'm twenty-four years old, and I was brought up on a lemon grove where I roamed wild. I'm pretty sure I can rock-climb.'

'Then let's go.'

As they clambered over rocks, discovered trickles of water and debated the difference between stalactites and stalagmites, he watched Holly, saw the lithe, sure grace with which she moved, the impatient pushing away of tendrils of blonde hair as they escaped her ponytail so that vibrant corn-coloured curls bounced off her shoulder.

As if she sensed his scrutiny, she smiled at him. 'You OK?'

'Yes.'

Somehow Holly had taken a bittersweet memory and created a new, happy one to blend with it. And he hoped that somewhere, somehow, his mother could see this, would know that he'd finally explored the caves.

For heaven's sake, Petrelli. Get a grip.

'Let's go eat—I've gone from ravenous to desperate!'

Once back on the beach, they unpacked the food: mini-quiches, tabbouleh salad, pork pies, tiny sandwiches, cheese straws and succulent Lycandrian olives, black and green and glistening in oil. They heaped their plates, sat back in the warmth of the sun and ate.

She shifted closer to him, turned to face him. Almost as if she had read his mind, she said, 'If Eloise could see you she'd be proud of you.'

The words cut him, threatened to destroy the warmth of the day, and as if on cue the sun hid behind a passing cloud.

Stefan shook his head. 'I don't think so.' If he'd been stronger, toughened up faster, jumped through the hoops his father had set, he could have saved her. *That* would have been something to be proud of.

'Well, *I* do.'

'Even if she would it wouldn't change anything.'

Not a single one of his achievements could change his mother's life and how it had panned out.

'The misery of her marriage, the horror of the custody battle, the fact that her love for me meant she suffered whatever my father meted out, her exile from Lycander...'

'That wasn't your fault. None of it.'

'If she hadn't loved me her life would have been a whole lot easier. Without me her life would have been immeasurably better.'

If he had been stronger, better, more princely, then her life would have been easier too. But he'd failed—or so his father had said. He had come in one day and announced the end of the regime. It was over and Eloise was gone.

In that moment, as he'd seen the cruelty on his father's face, Stefan had vowed that he would never be a prince—that as soon as he could he would follow his mother into exile. When he'd learnt of her death, in his grief and anger, he'd renewed that vow.

'I'm sorry.' Holly hesitated, then reached out and clasped his hand. 'Truly sorry. All I can say is please try to remember that she loved you and treasure the memories you have. I know she did.'

Stefan frowned, sure that alongside the compassion in her voice there was a strange wistfulness. As if she had a paucity of similar memories.

As if aware of it, she shifted slightly, turned to face the sea, choppier now, with white crests on the waves looping and rolling in the breeze, casting a salt scent towards the shore along with their spray.

She'd said her parents' marriage had been embittered, and she had hardly ever mentioned her mother.

'What happened with *your* parents?' He kept his voice gentle, non-intrusive.

'My mother left when I was eight—went to Australia.'

'That must have been tough. How did they sort out custody?'

'They didn't. She decided to make a clean break; I haven't seen her since.'

Now she turned to him.

'I know it's awful that your mother suffered, and it breaks my heart when I think about it. But I also know that you are so lucky that she loved

you. Because you see my mother never did—
never loved me. My parents wanted a boy. Desperately. After Eloise left, my father knew he
needed to get married—needed Romano heirs.
He was up-front with my mother, told that he
didn't love her, that his heart belonged to Eloise, but that he'd do his best to make her happy.
Maybe if they'd had a brood of children they
would have been. But it didn't happen, and as
time went by they became desperate. For a boy.
When Eloise had you I think it tipped my mother
over the edge—made her feel a complete failure. She did everything; she went to herbalists,
soothsayers, every doctor she could think of. I
think she would have sold her soul for a child—
or rather for a boy. When I turned up they were
devastated. I've heard people talking about it.'

Stefan scooted across the sand, moved as close
to her as possible and hoped his proximity would
offer some comfort. The idea of tiny baby Holly,
left unloved, desperate for care and love, made
his chest ache.

'My father hired a nurse…tried to persuade
my mother to take an interest. But she didn't.
I think she couldn't. It was as though the sight

of me turned her stomach. It always did and there's nothing I can do to change that. My father was different; his disappointment has never fully faded, but he has always shown me love and kindness and I will be grateful for ever for that.'

It explained so much about why Holly was willing to do anything for her father. Gratitude, a desire to make up for his disappointment in her gender and of course love. Confirmation, perhaps, that love gave power; if you accepted love then you had to give something back.

Next to him, she gave a sudden tight smile. 'Don't look so gutted—it could have been worse. My mother never physically hurt me, and there were plenty of staff around—they all looked out for me. And my father was amazing.'

She glanced at her watch.

'The tide is turning and the boat will soon be back for us. We'd better go.'

'Wait.'

Turning, he pulled her into his arms, rested her head against his shoulder, felt the tickle of her hair against his chin. For a second she resisted, and then she relaxed. He rubbed her back, hoped he could soothe her childhood pain.

They sat like that for a while and then she pulled back, touched his cheek with one gentle finger. 'We really do need to go.'

He nodded, rose and held out his hand to pull her up from the sand.

As they packed up the remains of their picnic a small voice warned him to take care. Holly had been rebuffed all her life by the person who should have loved her most and she was vulnerable.

But not to *him*, he reassured himself. Holly knew he wasn't a long-term prospect and she didn't even want him to be one. She'd been more than clear on that. But he knew that in this honeymoon period he wanted to make her happy, give her some memories to treasure.

They had a week—and he wanted to make it count.

CHAPTER THIRTEEN

HOLLY WOKE WITH a feeling of well-being and opened her eyes sleepily, aware of warmth, security and Stefan's arm around her. Her brain kicked in and computed the day. Already in countdown mode, she was aware that their honeymoon period was tick-tick-ticking away. But it was OK. They still had a few days to go.

Relief trickled through her and she closed her eyes—just as the alarm shrilled out and her brain properly kicked into gear, dissipating the cloud of sleep. She sat up.

Stefan made a small noise of disapproval, reached up and pulled her back down. The sleepy caress of his hands down her back caused the now familiar jolt of desire. But today she couldn't act on it. Instead she placed a gentle hand on his chest, leaned over and nuzzled his neck and then sat up again.

His eyes opened in protest.

'We have to get up,' she explained. 'Today we have somewhere we need to be.'

'Where?' Now alertness had come into play, and his grey eyes watched her.

Holly bit her lip. Part of her wanted to tell him, but another part suspected he'd refuse to go. 'I'd rather not say.'

Now he too sat up, leant back against the wooden headboard, and a frown grooved his forehead. 'I'd rather you did.'

Holly shook her head and plumped for honesty. 'You may not go if I do.'

'And you want me to go?'

'Yes.'

A pause, and then he shrugged. 'Then we'll go.'

'Thank you.' She dropped a kiss on the top of his head and grinned at him. 'I'm going to get ready.'

'Lumberjack look or suit?'

'Lumberjack is fine, and there won't be any reporters. Or I hope not.'

Now she frowned. Despite promises from the press that they would respect their privacy, April had been correct. Stray reporters dogged their steps. Not many, to be fair, but enough that they had taken to sneaking out through the back door of the hotel en route to quirky corners of Lycander, where they wandered hand in hand, eating ice cream, or savoury crêpes, chatting or walking in silence. But even then every so often she'd been aware of the click of a camera, the sense of being followed.

'OK. Let's get this show on the road.'

Swinging her legs out of bed, she headed for the bathroom, trying to soothe the jangle of nerves, her anxiety that she was making a monumental mistake—a massive overstepping of the bounds of their marriage deal.

Stefan looked out of the window of the official car, watching as the prosperous vista dropped away and the houses became progressively more dingy, the vegetation more sparse and scrubby, the poverty more and more clear. He realised they were headed to the now familiar outskirts—back to the suburb they had first visited, where they had met Sasha.

The car glided to a stop near the nursery, and once again the sheer contrast between life here and in the affluent city hit him anew. Roofless houses, patched over with tin, smashed windows... And yet a community resided here. Children were playing in the streets, looking at the cars with rapt interest.

Cars in the plural... Another car from the royal fleet was parked opposite.

The door opened and he watched with a sense of inevitability as Frederick emerged, flanked by two security men whom he waved away to a discreet distance.

The Crown Prince's expression mirrored his own—surprise mixed with resignation—and a sense of solidarity sneaked up on Stefan. Seconds later Sunita also stepped out, clad in a discreet dark blue dress. His sister-in-law waved cheerily and Stefan lifted a hand in an attempt at enthusiasm.

'Why are we here?' he hissed out of the side of his mouth.

Holly gave him a tentative smile, though her blue eyes shaded apprehensively. 'You'll see. Come on.'

Compression banded his chest and the sense that he had been manipulated fuzzed his brain as he considered his options. He could ask Franco to turn the car and rev it out of here. But wiser counsel prevailed—that would hardly back up the impression of brothers reunited. Whilst there were no reporters visible, he was pretty sure this meeting could hardly be kept secret.

A glance at Frederick indicated that he'd come to much the same conclusion, and he headed towards them as Stefan climbed out, no doubt propelled by a prod in the back from Sunita.

'Stefan,' he said formally.

'Freddy.'

Stefan couldn't resist. His brother had hated being called Freddy as a child, and the sense of being pushed into an awkward position had clearly sent Stefan straight back to childhood. Any minute now he'd find a pram and start chucking toys.

To his surprise, Frederick's face split into an unexpected smile.

'No one's called me that since you left,' he said. 'And, for the record, this wasn't my idea. At a guess, it wasn't yours either.'

'Nope.' *Damn right.*

'Then we've been ambushed.' Frederick turned

and smiled affably at his wife. 'Perhaps you want to enlighten us as to why we're here?'

'Actually, this is Holly's show. I am merely her assistant—or accomplice, depending on how you want to look at it. Holly, over to you.'

Holly's show. The words pulled the band tighter round his chest. Since his father, it had never been anyone's show but Stefan's own. Warning bells clanged as he focused on her, watched as she straightened up, pushed a tendril of hair behind her ear and divided her focus between Frederick and himself.

'This community has been hard-hit. It was already in trouble and the storm made things worse. What you both have in common is a desire to right the wrongs and injustices your father committed and help make Lycander a better place. I thought maybe you could work together on this specific community—use the ideas and strengths you both have. Frederick, I know how much you care about education. And, Stefan, I know of your belief in social housing. Together you could build houses…schools. I know you are doing that throughout Lycander, but perhaps this could be the one place that represents Stefan's return to Lycander. If that makes sense. What do you think?'

She held her ground in the silence that followed.

Frederick glanced at his wife and Stefan could sense some sort of silent communication in progress. He suspected Sunita was issuing an escape route veto. Well, she had that right. Holly didn't.

In reality escape wasn't possible—this community *did* need assistance and he could provide it. But, right or wrong, the whole scenario didn't sit well with him. Holly had pushed him onto the moral high ground—was pulling his strings, pushing his buttons. *Find the cliché and apply.*

So it might be. But these people in this community had been pushed into poverty and destitution by the policies his father had instigated. His father had pushed buttons and pulled strings to cause dissension and unhappiness. He knew Holly's motives were good, that her aim was to help sow accord and not discord, and to achieve help for this place and the people who lived in it. Yet he couldn't shake the warning buzz in his head, the shades of discomfort.

But that was for later. Here and now, this was a project he believed in.

'I'm in.' He turned to his brother. 'But don't feel you have to do this—I can handle it solo.'

Impossible to guess the thoughts that were going through Frederick's blond head, but his face lightened into a smile. 'Actually, I think this *should* be a joint enterprise. I know it's your honeymoon, but do you want to stick around here for a bit and have a look? Bounce some ideas.'

One deep breath and then Stefan nodded. 'Sure.'

In unison, Sunita and Holly stepped forward.

'Grand!' Sunita said. 'Holly and I will take one car and you boys can have the other. Have fun!'

Holly paced the hotel room, anxiety edging her nerves as she wondered how it was going—whether this project would bring the brothers together. She wondered if she'd misread Stefan's body language, the sense of irritation at her perceived interference. Yet she couldn't regret it.

Her phone buzzed and she snatched it up, tried not be disappointed at the identity of the caller.

'Hi, April.'

'Holly. That's a *great* write-up on you and Stefan. That should definitely nail it with regard to everyone buying into the two of you.'

Huh?

'I haven't heard of the reporter but it's a fair article—she did well.'

Still not with it, she held her phone in place with her shoulder and pulled her laptop towards her. Pulled up the article April was describing in happy detail.

Oh, hell.

'April, I'll call you back.'

Disconnecting, she sank onto the armchair and started to read.

Love for Real? The Verdict is In.

As all of Lycander knows, last week Prince Stefan tied the knot with Holly Romano, and amid a complicated backdrop of wills and lemons, the big question has been: Are they in love for real?

Well, let's take a look at some of the evidence.

Exhibit One: The official interview done by April Fotherington —aka wife of Chief Advi-

sor Marcus Alriksson—accompanied by the first official photograph.

Analysis: A little posed, a little formal, expressions a little strained. But who can blame them? It's hard to pose officially.

Verdict: Are they in love? Possibly...maybe.

Exhibit Two: The televised interview.

Analysis: They talked the talk, walked the walk...until it came to the L question. Then they stumbled, but made a quick recovery.

Verdict: Are they in love? Maybe, baby.

Exhibit Three: The wedding.

Analysis: Definitely looking hot—but who wouldn't in a dress like that?

Verdict: The jury is still out.

So I undertook a little casual surveillance...

Please note that I made no attempt to breach the privacy of the honeymoon suite itself, but I am guilty of a bit of ducking and diving whilst I followed the newlyweds around Lycander.

And so to Exhibit Four:

Holly's heart hit her boots as she skimmed the photos.

Herself in the palace gardens, looking up at

Stefan, a smile on her lips and love in her eyes. *Jeez*. She looked as if she thought he was the best thing since sliced granary. Oh, and joy! There was a picture of them in a clinch. She was literally hanging off his lips. But it wasn't only that photo. The next was the killer. Her hand was on his T-shirt, brushing off a speck of dirt, and the goddamn look in her eyes was one of love.

She didn't need to read the verdict, but she did it anyway—just in case there was even a sliver of a possibility that she'd got it wrong.

Verdict: One loved-up princess...
So, the best of luck to our new royals. Life gave them lemons and it looks like Princess Holly is going to make lemonade!

Panic strummed every single synapse—how had it happened? This reporter had got it *right*. Somewhere down the line she'd fallen for Stefan. Fool that she was. He'd made it more than clear that he was no fairy tale prince and she'd been damned sure her fairy tale days were over. Yet somehow she'd done it again—fallen in love with a man who didn't love her back.

What to do? *What to do?*

For a start she had to make sure Stefan didn't so much as suspect the truth. If he saw this article she'd laugh it off, put it down to the light, her acting skills, sexual afterglow...anything but the truth.

Speak of the devil... She looked up as the door opened, braced herself, shut the laptop and rose to her feet.

'Hi. How did it go?' *Too breezy.*

'It went fine.'

His voice was even—not cold, but not warm, and the glint she'd become used to over the past days was gone. She'd been right—he was mad at her.

'Good—and I'm sorry.'

'For what?' He shrugged off his jacket and threw it over the back of an armchair.

'I know I forced your hand. I didn't think you'd go if I'd told you where we were going.'

Even as she focused on the words the truth whirled inside her head, made his coolness hurt more. *Love...* She *loved* him.

'It should have been my decision to make. I don't like being bulldozed or manipulated. But I do understand that you did it with the best intentions, and Frederick and I had a productive few hours. The community wins…brand Petrelli Princes wins.'

'That isn't why I organised it.'

'Then why *did* you?'

'Because I knew you and Frederick weren't bonding and I wanted to give you a chance to sort it out, to bring you closer together, to show you how much you have in common. I thought you could both let go of the past by doing something worthwhile together *now*. If you can let go of the past then you have a future.'

She could only pray that he didn't read the subtext she was seeing herself. Damn it, she wanted a future with this man. Wanted him to decide love was for him after all.

'The past makes us who we are,' he said. 'The past matters—you can't just let go of it. But you can learn from it.'

'But maybe sometimes the lessons we learn from it are wrong. Sunita told me that your father pitted you and Frederick against each other; it was Alphonse who fostered the dislike. You and Frederick can overcome that.'

His grey eyes darkened, and bleak shadows

chased across them as he shook his head. 'If it were as easy as that perhaps we could. But it isn't. In any case, I don't want closeness with Frederick.'

'Why not?'

'That's not my way, Holly. I prefer to walk alone. I like the control it gives me to do what I want to do without answering to anyone else.'

The certainty in his voice was unassailable, and his words made her heart ache as she began to accept the futility of her love.

But maybe she could make him see reason.

'You can still have control and be close to others—you would still have choices.' *Deep breath.* 'I know how much seeing your mother suffer must have hurt you, and I know it must feel like it was your fault...that loving you resulted in hurt for her.'

'It didn't *feel* like that. That is what *happened.* Fact, not feeling.'

'But *all* love doesn't have to be like that. Your mother wouldn't want you to give up on closeness or love. I know that.'

'Then she would be wrong. She had one life, Holly. One life—and most of it was miserable because of her love for *me*. She was chained to an abusive man who used her love for me to humiliate her, to make her life hell. Her love for me gave my father power. Love gives power.'

Oh, God. As her brain joined the dots all she wanted to do was hold him, but as she moved towards him she saw him move imperceptibly backwards and she stopped.

'And your love for her...it gave your father power over *you*?'

'Yes.' His voice was flat. 'And he used that power. He made me pay dearly for every visit to my mother. He decided her love for me had weakened me, made me less "princely". So he devised a regime—a training programme. If I adhered to it, if I achieved his goals, I'd get time with my mother—as well as becoming a *real* prince, of course.'

The sneer, the bitterness, made her ache even as she was appalled at Alphonse's actions. It twisted her insides. The image of a young boy, desperately missing his mother, being put through such a regime made her feel ill.

'But even then he changed the rules. One day

the regime was over. I'd failed and my mother
was gone. Exiled.'

'But…*why*?' It seemed impossible to fathom
how anyone could do that.

'He'd met his next wife. She wanted rid of Eloise. He wanted it to look as though she'd abandoned me and he was remarrying to give his
children a "proper" mother. It worked for him.
And love *still* gave him power—over both of us.
My mother went without a fight because she was
scared of what he might do to me. As for me,
there was nothing I could do—I'd already failed
her.'

'No!' The word was torn from her, and now she
did move towards him—didn't care if he rejected
her. She stepped into his space and put her arms
around him. 'That's not true.'

But she could see exactly why his younger self
had thought that—knew that deep down, despite
his adult understanding, he still believed it. His
body was hard, unyielding, no trace of the man
she'd shared so much passion with, the man who
had held her, whose arms she had woken up in
these past three mornings.

'Just like it's not my fault that my mother

didn't—couldn't—love me. That wasn't *my* failure. I was a child. So were you. You didn't fail your mother.'

She held her breath, and then hope deflated as he shrugged.

'Whether it's true or not isn't the point. I don't want closeness. Closeness leads to love. Love is not for me—I won't give anyone that power again. Hell, I don't want that power over anyone either.'

That told her. Any not yet formed idea of telling him of her love died before it could even take root. She could not, *would* not, repeat the past. He was right—the past was there to be learned from.

Her mother, her father, *his* mother, *his* father, had all been caught in the coils of unrequited love. It had caused bitterness and misery and she was damned if she would walk that path. Or do that to him. Because if he even so much as suspected she'd fallen for him he would be appalled, and she couldn't stand the humiliation of that.

She loved him—he didn't love her. She would not do what her mother had done: hang on for years, becoming progressively more bitter, hoping in perpetuity that he would miraculously change his mind and love her. The only path—the only *sensible* path—was to walk away. At speed, with as much dignity as possible.

Think.

She couldn't walk away from their marriage—ironically those vows *did* bind them for another few months—but she could change the terms of the deal. That was a language Stefan *did* understand. Because she couldn't have any sort of relationship with him—not now she knew she loved him.

'I don't agree,' she said simply. 'Love doesn't have to give abusive power. Look at Sunita and Frederick. Look at Marcus and April.'

'That is the choice they have made. It's not a choice I agree with.'

'And that's your right. Just like it's your right and choice not to engage with Frederick. But you're missing out. Yes, you won't get hurt, but you won't experience closeness either.' Another deep breath and she forced herself to continue. 'On that note, I think we need to cool it.'

His eyes registered shock, surprise and a fleeting emotion that looked like hurt, and for an instant she nearly changed her mind. But Stefan

did not love her; he would never love her. Right
now, she had to protect herself.

'Why?' he asked.

Another deep breath. 'There's an article about
us.' Her gaze flicked to the laptop. 'It's on there,
if you want to look.'

Bracing herself, she waited as he flipped the
screen up, scanned the article. Then his grey eyes
came up to study her.

Hold it together. She wouldn't, *couldn't* allow
the humiliation of letting him know what a fool
she had been.

'It made me realise that I *do* want the real thing
one day—a real marriage with love. So what we
are doing feels wrong to me. I want to call it a
day now, instead of in a few days. No big deal,
right?'

Stefan's expression was unreadable, though she
could see the tension in the jut of his jaw, the almost unnatural stillness of his body.

'No big deal,' he agreed, his voice without any
discernible emotion.

No big deal. A hollow feeling of being bereft
scooped her insides. She'd never feel his touch
again, never hold him, never wake up in the crook

of his arm, never walk hand in hand with him. *Never*... The word that rhymed with *for ever* and it meant the opposite. Her heartache deepened and her whole being scrambled to find some semblance of pride.

He must not suspect the truth.

CHAPTER FOURTEEN

STEFAN EYED HIS brother over the piles of reports that littered the table between them, tried to focus on the figures before him. Lord knew they were important. The community project had grown and developed over the past few days of discussion. Days when they had found common beliefs and causes, a mutual desire to help those less fortunate, to give something back.

Yet despite the importance of the documents on the table it took all his willpower to focus, to try and block the images of Holly that invaded his brain wherever he was.

It shouldn't matter—he shouldn't miss her so damn much. Shouldn't keep wanting to talk to her, tell her about the project. Shouldn't miss the warmth of her body next to his in the night. Shouldn't miss the sound of her laughter, the way she swirled a tendril of her hair, the tantalising *Holly*-ness of her.

Frederick closed the lid of his computer. 'I think we should finish up for today.' A hesitation and then, 'I know Holly is at Il Boschetto di Sole for a few days—I hope her father is OK?'

'He's fine.' His illness was a cover story to explain Holly's absence.

'Sunita's out for the evening. Would you like to come back to the palace? Have a beer…spend some time with Amil. I know he'd like that.' Another pause. 'And so would I.'

Stefan opened his mouth, closed it again. He realised the idea appealed—that the idea of a return to the hotel where Holly's absence was like an actual physical pain didn't.

'That would be good. Thank you.'

Twenty minutes later he entered Frederick and Sunita's home, watching as Amil hurtled across the floor away from the nanny and into Frederick's outstretched arms with a cry of, 'Daddy!'

Stefan stood still, aware of a pang that smote him. A pang of what? Envy? Surely not—this was exactly what he *didn't* want.

Frederick thanked the nanny before she left and then grinned at his son. 'Today Uncle Stefan is here for your bath.'

Amil beamed at him and Stefan's heart gave a funny little twist. Twisted further as he ended up in the bathroom, sleeves rolled up, sitting by the tub where Amil sat, four rubber ducks bobbing in the water.

'Sing the song, Uncle Stefan.'

Stefan shook his head. 'I don't know it, Amil. I'm sorry.'

'Yes, you do. Eloise and I sang it to you in *your* bath,' Frederick said from the doorway, and started to hum.

The tune ricocheted around his brain...evoked a crystal-clear memory. Himself in the bath, surrounded by bubbles, a rubber duck in each hand, splashing in time as his mother and Frederick sang.

'"Five little ducks went swimming one day..."'

Soon he and Frederick were singing and Amil was splashing and moving the ducks around the bath. Finally Frederick called a halt, helped Amil out of the bath, wrapped him in a fluffy towel and carried him into the lounge.

'Help yourself to a drink whilst I put Amil to bed.'

'Uncle Stefan. Please read my book?'

Frederick hesitated, then glanced at Stefan with a rueful smile. 'Do you mind?'

'Not at all.'

And he meant it. So he read his nephew a book featuring a variety of farmyard animals and felt his heart tug again.

Later, when Amil was in bed, Frederick poured two glasses of deep red wine and heated up a casserole. He sat down opposite Stefan in the spacious kitchen as the scent of herbs filled the air. 'Can we talk?'

'Sure.' Though wariness touched him.

'I know the deal you made with Marcus. Support me and get your lands back. I went along with it because I knew you wouldn't accept the lands otherwise. But I have always been happy to restore them; they are yours by right. I want you to know that.'

Stefan shook his head. 'I don't work like that. Our father took my rights and my lands away— that was his right. I would like them back, but I have no wish to be beholden.'

'We're brothers. You wouldn't be beholden. It wouldn't give me any power over you. That's what you're worried about, isn't it? Giving anyone power over you. Me? Holly?'

Stefan froze. 'Holly has nothing to do with this.'

'Yes, she does. You made a deal with her too—a marriage deal. And now I think you care about her. Maybe even love her.'

'Of course I don't. I don't *do* love.' Inside him something twisted, turned, unlocked with a creak, opening a floodgate of panic.

His brother smiled. 'Famous last words, little brother. Sometimes love doesn't give you a choice.'

'There is *always* a choice.' And right now he chose to cut himself loose before it was too late to uproot love. Love that had already coiled around his heart, inserting insidious tendrils of weakness.

Whoa… *Love?* He *loved* Holly…? *Loved* her?

Frederick leant forward, his blue eyes arresting, his mien serious. 'This may be none of my business, but you are my brother. We shared a childhood…we shared an upbringing. I cared about your mother and I cared about you. But when Eloise left, when you still got to see her and I didn't, I was angry and I blamed you. Instead of becoming a better brother I switched off, insulated myself from all emotions and feelings, allowed our father to mess with my head. Like I know he messed with yours. I owe you an apology, Stefan; I didn't step up when I should have.'

Stefan could feel emotions long-buried begin to surface. The hurt he'd felt at losing Frederick's affection…the guilt of his belief that he'd deserved to lose it…their father's relentless pitting of brother against brother. But through it all he hadn't thought about how *Frederick* felt, how *he* was affected.

'Maybe it's time to put it behind us.'

He saw an image of Holly's face, heard an echo of her voice. *'If you can let go of the past then you can have a future.'*

'Go forward from here.'

'I'd like that.' Frederick took a breath. 'But there's something else I'd like to say. Our father messed with my head so much I didn't believe that I could be a good husband or father. Sunita and Amil showed me that I can—maybe Holly can show you the same. Don't let our father mess with your head from beyond the grave.

If you love her, go for it—I promise you it will be worth it.'

Frederick paused and leant over and ruffled Stefan's hair. The gesture was ridiculously familiar.

'Lecture over, little bro, but if you need anything then let me know.'

Stefan stood up, unsure of what to say. He loved Holly—and now he had a choice as to what to do about it.

Holly looked up from her computer as her father knocked on the door, a look of concern on his face. 'Holly, Jessica has made dinner. It will be ready in half an hour—come eat something.'

'I'm sorry, Dad. I'm just not hungry. But you two go ahead.' Holly summoned up a smile. 'I'm glad it's working out with Jessica.'

'That is thanks to Stefan.' Thomas uttered the name with caution. 'It was he who spoke with me, persuaded me to talk to Jessica.'

'He did?' Holly looked up. She knew she shouldn't encourage the conversation—she was trying to forget Stefan—yet she wanted to know.

'Yes, he did. In fact my temporary son-in-law was quite vocal on the subject.'

'He was?' Holly tried to feel annoyed. Instead all she could summon was a picture of Stefan— the jut of his jaw, the intensity of his eyes, the gentle touch of his hand, his smile.

'Yes, and what he said made me think.'

Her father entered the room and sat down on the bed, just as he had when she was younger, studying for exams.

'I owe you an apology.'

'No. You don't.' Now she really *was* annoyed. 'And if Stefan told you that I hope you told him to get knotted.'

'He said nothing so discourteous and neither did I. What he *did* tell me about was about your job prospects at Lamberts. Something *you* hadn't told me.'

'Because it's not important.'

'Yes, Holly, it *is* important. You should have told me—but also I should have asked. Instead I assumed that you wanted what I wanted, that your wish was to live here with me, marry, settle down, have Romano heirs, and of course work here on Il Boschetto di Sole. I assumed all that and that was wrong.'

'No, Papa. It wasn't wrong. Our family has worked here for generations. I do want to work here—of course I do.'

'But it doesn't have to be *now*, Holly. You need time to spread your wings, see the world, travel. Yes, of course I want you to live here, settle down, but most of all I want you to be happy. I can look after Il Boschetto di Sole and I can also look after myself. That is *my* responsibility. I want to be here to see your children and I will do my best to do so. I am sure Jessica will help me do that.'

Holly stood up, moved over to her father and hugged him. 'Thank you.'

'Now, come and eat with us and tell us about the new job. I want to know all about it.'

Holly grinned at him, and for a moment her heart lightened. But before she could say anything more there was another knock on the door and Jessica popped her head round, looking flustered.

'We have a visitor.'

'Who?'

'Prince Stefan. I've put him in the lounge.'

Holly's heart jumped as her tummy went into freefall.

Her father rose to his feet and smiled. 'Go to him, Holly.'

'I can't. Tell him I'm not here—that I'm sick, have been beamed up by aliens… Anything!'

Her father shook his head. 'Do you love him?'

She flinched. 'Of course not. You know that this is a marriage of convenience.'

'Are you sure?'

Holly tried to hold his gaze, but couldn't.

'Love is nothing to be ashamed of,' her father said gently.

'I'm not ashamed.' Holly twisted her hands together, saw the love in her father's eyes and opted for the truth. 'But Stefan doesn't want my love. He doesn't want anyone's love. I was a fool to fall for him. All I want to do now is get over it.'

'Have you told him you love him?'

'No! And I'm not going to. There is no point in humiliating myself and making him feel bad. This is not his fault.' Unlike Graham, Stefan had not strung her along or pretended love—

he'd been up-front. 'I don't want to be like you and my mother.'

Thomas closed his eyes for a moment, then opened them, reached out and touched her arm. 'Holly. Please do not let me and your mother's actions destroy your relationship or taint your attitude to love. Our mistakes, our issues, do not need to be yours. Stefan is not me, and you are not your mother. Give your love a chance.'

Holly looked at him and her own words to Stefan came back to her. *If you can let go of the past then you can have a future.* And his words, about the past being there to be learned from.

What if they were both right?

What if her father was right?

Maybe she *should* let go of her past and tell Stefan of her love. And if he rejected that love then she would learn from her parents and she would walk away, knowing she had done all she could to give love a chance.

'Thank you, Papa.' She dropped a kiss on his head and then, pulling up every reserve of courage, she headed for the lounge.

As she entered her heart pounded so hard it was a wonder her ribcage could cope. Her lungs certainly couldn't. Her breath caught in her throat as she saw him, standing by the mantelpiece, studying the array of photographs there, his whole body tense.

His fingers drummed his thigh as he turned to face her. 'Holly. We need to talk.'

What to say? What to say? And where to say it?

Not here. Somehow she wanted to be outside, under the sky, amongst the trees in the vast beauty of Il Boschetto di Sole.

'Shall we go outside?'

He nodded, and together they made their way to the front door and stepped out into the early evening, where the last rays of sunshine were giving way to the dusk. His proximity made her head whirl, and his familiar scent made her want to bury herself in his arms and burrow in.

Rather than that, she sought some form of conversation. 'So…um…how is it going with Frederick?'

'Good. We've come up with some pretty solid ideas that we're both excited about.'

'Good.'

Conversation dwindled after that as they walked through the garden of the villa and headed by tacit consent to the lemon groves, where the intense fragrance offered her the comfort of familiarity as they wended through the trees towards a bench. A breeze holding the first chill of the year blew and she gave a small shiver.

'Here.' He shrugged off the green and blue checked shirt that he wore over a deep blue T-shirt. Seeing his bare arms made her shiver with the sudden bittersweet ache of desire and the memory of being held. Perhaps she should refuse the shirt, but she couldn't. She wanted to feel the material that had touched his skin against hers.

'Thank you.'

They sat on the bench and she turned to him, knowing she needed to do it—take the plunge.

'I'm glad you're here. I need to talk to you. We left some things unsaid.'

The ghost of a smile touched his lips. 'Yes, we did. That's why I'm here too. To say…'

Goodbye? Had he discovered some legal loophole that would allow their marriage to be annulled?

'Could I go first? Please.' Before she bottled it.

For a moment she thought, almost hoped, he'd refuse, but then he nodded. 'Go ahead.'

After a deep breath she launched in. 'I wasn't fully truthful with you and I should have been. But before I say what I need to say I need you to know that this is not your fault.'

Come on, Holly.

'I love you.'

There—she'd said it. Admittedly whilst staring down at the slats of the wooden bench, but she'd said it.

She hurried on. 'I just wanted you to know. I don't want anything back…don't expect anything back. And please don't feel bad—I don't regret loving you.'

'Holly.' His voice sounded strangled. 'Look at me.'

She looked up, braced herself for pity, anger, sorrow, but instead saw a shell-shocked look of stunned disbelief succeeded by a dawning of joy, a light so bright, so happy, that her own heart gave a small cautious leap.

'I came here to tell you *I* love *you*.'

Happiness sparked, but she doused the joy, needed to know he meant it, that it was real and not an illusion.

'Don't say it because you feel sorry for me.'

'I would never do that. I do not feel sorry for you. I love you.'

'But just days ago you told me you didn't want love...didn't *do* love.'

'It turns out I knew absolutely nothing about love. I love you whether I want to or not, and it turns out I *do* want to.' He sounded almost bewildered. 'I love you and I want to shout it from the rooftops. I love the way you smile, I love the way you twirl your hair round your finger, I love your warmth, your generosity, your loyalty and how much you care. Loving you makes me a better person—a stronger person, not a weaker one. Maybe it does give you power over me, but I trust you not to abuse that power. I've been falling for you since the moment I laid eyes on you; and now you have made me the happiest man on this earth.'

Now he paused.

'As long as you're sure too. You're not mistaking love for duty? It's not for your father, or for Il Boschetto di Sole, or...?'

'No! This love is for real! I love you—I love how you bring out the best in me, make me strive and question and leave my comfort zone. You make me smile, you make me laugh, you make me feel safe, you encourage me and you make me so happy I can feel the happiness tingle through my whole body.'

He rose to his feet and pulled her up with him. He spanned her waist with his hands and twirled her round, and then he sank to one knee and took her hand in his.

'In this beautiful place—*our* beautiful place— will you, Holly Romano, stay married to me, Stefan Petrelli, for ever? To have and to hold, till death us do part?'

She beamed. 'Yes, I will.'

And as he stood and kissed her, she knew that they would fulfil each and every vow they had made with love and happiness. For ever.

EPILOGUE

STEFAN LOOKED OUT over Forester's Glade—
Radura dei Guardaboschi.

'You OK?' Holly asked, slipping her hand into
his.

'Yes. Really I am.'

They had just scattered his mother's ashes over
the earth she had loved so much and a sense of
peace enveloped him.

'I hope she is now at rest.'

Holly moved even closer to him, increased the
pressure of her clasp. 'I wish I could have known
her. I wish it could all have panned out differently.'

'Me too. But I know she would have been happy
for me and I know she would have loved you. Not,
of course, as much as I do, but she would have
loved you.'

For a moment they looked out over the lush,
verdant land, listening to the babble of the stream,
the rush of the waterfall.

'I love you very much, Holly. And I am very proud of you. Especially for that award.'

'I'm pretty stoked myself.'

She'd won Global Marketing Trainee of the Year and she more than deserved it.

'But the wonderful thing is how much I love the work. And did you see my father's face when they handed me the prize?'

'I thought he'd burst, he was so proud.'

She nestled closer to him. 'I wouldn't have tried it if it wasn't for you.'

'Well, I wouldn't have such a great relationship with Frederick if it wasn't for you.'

His closeness with his older brother made him feel warm inside. He knew Frederick would always have his back and vice versa.

'I guess we work pretty well together, huh?'

'I guess we do.'

Turning, he pulled her into his arms and knew that this marriage deal was one that would last for ever—and it was the best deal he'd ever made.

* * * * *

LET'S TALK

Romance

For exclusive extracts, competitions
and special offers, find us online:

f facebook.com/millsandboon

⊙ @millsandboonuk

🐦 @millsandboon

Or get in touch on 0844 844 1351*

For all the latest titles coming soon,
visit millsandboon.co.uk/nextmonth